I BURN FOR YOU

MORE RAVES FOR THE WORK OF SUSAN SIZEMORE

The critics love
these bestselling books from
SUSAN SIZEMORE

PRIMAL HEAT
New York Times and *USA Today* bestseller

"An intriguing alternate reality with absorbing characters and touches of humor makes this series one of the best and most consistently appealing around."

—*Romantic Times*

"Passion, danger, and mystery fill the pages of *Primal Heat* . . . an intense and satisfying read."

—Romance Reviews Today

"This world grows more fascinating as each new chapter unfolds. Politics, power, mystery, and romance make for a heady combination . . ."

—Huntress Reviews

MASTER OF DARKNESS
New York Times and *USA Today* bestseller

"What a bad boy charmer! Definitely Sizemore's most fun and original hero to date. . . . Once again, Sizemore serves up a terrific blend of edgy humor, passionate romance, and thrilling danger."

—*Romantic Times*

"Great action, snappy dialogue and powerful prose. . . . Susan Sizemore's *Master of Darkness* is engaging from beginning to incredible end."

—A Romance Review

Primal Needs

SUSAN SIZEMORE

POCKET STAR BOOKS
New York   London   Toronto   Sydney

Pocket Star Books
A Division of Simon & Schuster, Inc.
1230 Avenue of the Americas
New York, NY 10020

This book is a work of fiction. Names, characters, places, and incidents either are products of the author's imagination or are used fictitiously. Any resemblance to actual events or locales or persons, living or dead, is entirely coincidental.

First Pocket Star Books paperback edition January 2009

POCKET STAR BOOKS and colophon are registered trademarks of Simon & Schuster, Inc.

For information about special discounts for bulk purchases, please contact Simon & Schuster Special Sales at 1-800-456-6798 or business@simonandschuster.com.

Cover design by Lisa Litwack. Photo of woman by Shirley Green.

Manufactured in the United States of America

10 9 8 7 6 5 4 3 2 1

ISBN-13: 978-1-4165-6212-2
ISBN-10:   1-4165-6212-5

For Ethan Ellenberg

Chapter One

December 12
San Diego, CA
Clan Wolf Citadel

"Charles? What kind of name is Charles for a vampire?"

Sid knew that her brother was trying to distract her as they waited in Matri Juanita's moonwashed garden. A faint glow lit the sky to the east of San Diego, the result of another wildfire in the mountains. At least the wind was blowing the far-off ash and smoke away from the city.

To show she appreciated Laurent's effort, she went along with the distraction. "We've had this discussion for nearly two years. I like the name Charles. It's a nice, normal name."

"Laurent's a nice, normal name," Laurent said.

"No, it isn't."

"It is for a vampire."

"What would you prefer I named him?" she asked.

"Something with gravitas. Something suitable—"

"For melodrama?" she interrupted. "I'm sick of melodrama."

"Melodrama comes with the territory, kid. What about changing his name to Anthony?"

Sid laughed. "Oh, please! Our mother is named Antonia. My sire is named Anthony. Your own daughter is Antonia Junior."

"We call her Toni. Your kid's going to be called Chuck, you know. Chuck the Vampire. I shudder to think of it."

"What about Charlie the Vampire?" she asked.

"Almost as bad."

It had been a long time since Sid had been in this garden. The scent of night-blooming flowers brought back a lot of memories. She noticed that her fingers were twined tightly together in her lap and made a conscious effort to relax. She glanced at the house. "What's taking so long? Shouldn't they be ready by now? And why do we even have to do this in the first place?"

They were taking her baby from her, and she hated them.

Laurent put his hand over hers. "You know that this is for the best. You can't deal with Charles on your own once his fangs come out."

Mortals had no idea how terrible the terrible twos could really be. She wished she'd had a daughter. Not only did their kind need more females if they were going to remain a viable species, but young vampire females didn't turn into bloodlusting animals when their baby fangs first came in.

Testosterone poisoning started early among vampire males, and the aggression needed to be controlled, channeled. Young males needed to be civilized if they were to mature into sane Primes. They needed drill sergeants more than they did doting mothers. Or so Sid had always believed, until her own son came along. Generation upon generation of vampire mothers had been through this. The ceremony this evening was supposed to reassure her that the finest care would be taken of her baby, but . . .

"You weren't raised in a crèche," Sid reminded Laurent. "Mom dealt just fine with you. You turned out okay. Eventually."

"Eventually." There was no humor in the sound when he laughed. "Antonia did the best she could when she had the chance to be near me. But remember that she was a prisoner, and that I was mostly raised among a pack of Tribe young where the rule is kill or be killed. Sometimes I doubted I would make it out alive. The Clans created a safe, structured environment for our little monsters. This is best for Charles, and for you."

Sid sighed. "I'm not fighting the necessity of sending my baby away, but I hate it."

He patted her hand. "Every parent hates it."

This reminder didn't make the pain of loss any easier, but it did reinforce the necessity of this custom.

The sound of a door sliding open drew their attention and they both stood as Lady Juanita's bondmate gestured.

"Please come with me, Laurent," he said. "Please wait a few moments longer, Lady Sidonie." He bowed very formally to her, then disappeared back into the house.

"If he knew you better he wouldn't call you a lady," Laurent said.

It was the sort of lame joke brothers were supposed to make. She was called Lady Sidonie because providing the Wolf Clan with a child made her head of her own House.

"Go on in," she told Laurent. "Maybe you can get them to hurry up with this stupid ceremony.

Why does Lady Juanita have to be so damn formal anyway?"

He gave her a reassuring kiss on the cheek before he left her alone in the garden.

It was only after Sid was by herself that the memories of the last time she'd been by this bench, in front of this fountain, came rushing back.

Three Years Ago

"I've been looking for you, Sidonie," Joe Bleythin said.

Sid stood. The moment she'd dreaded had finally arrived. "I thought you might be."

Joe said, "Lucy, you got some 'splainin' to do."

If he could joke, maybe this wouldn't be as bad as she thought. The meeting of vampires and werefolk earlier in the evening had brought out some startling revelations about the entwined histories of their species. It had also left open questions about her and Joe's relationship that Sid was reluctant to discuss.

"What can I say?" Sid asked. "I'm as surprised as you are to find out that vampires and werewolves can mate."

"Do you know that you blink when you lie?"

"I do not!"

Joe gave a harsh laugh. The air around them seemed to grow colder. "So you are lying."

Her werewolf knew her too well—except for the things she'd made him forget. Sid turned away. "I do not want to have this conversation with you, Joseph Bleythin. At least not here and now."

"What do you know?" he demanded. "When did you know it? And for how long? And just what haven't you been telling me?"

"About the Hunyaras? I don't know any more than you do about the bad guy's claims about Cathy's family coming from a werewolf having children with a vampire." That much was true, even if . . .

"Your species didn't seem repulsed by the idea of mating with members of my species when the subject came up. Why was I the one who protested?"

Sid shrugged. "Well, you know Primes. Vampire males see it as their right to have sex with anything that takes their fancy. But—"

"What about vampire females? What about you?"

"What about *me*?"

"How much have you lied to me about us? Why?"

His anger was shredding her. "It's complicated." She sighed. "Maybe the lesson is to never do anything for anyone else's own good, because it'll only come back and bite you on the ass."

"Explain that to me."

"Okay." She looked up at the moon rather than at Joe. "I love you."

He was silent for a long time, and she couldn't bear to look at him. She heard him pace around the fountain, then come back to her.

"I don't love you," he said.

Sid made herself look him in the eye. "Yes, you do. You just don't remember."

"What are you talking about?"

"We've been lovers, Joe. I made you forget."

After that, the shouting started.

When it was over, her life might as well have been, too.

Chapter Two

Present Day

"*Y*ou're thinking about Joe, aren't you?"

Sid didn't know when her sister-in-law had come to sit beside her. The former vampire hunter moved quietly for a mortal. "How can you tell? You're not telepathic, Eden."

"I know that miserable look. It's not Charles that was on your mind just now."

Eden was the only person to whom Sid had confided the details of the incredible disaster she'd made out of her relationship with Joe Bleythin. Even then, she'd only told Eden because her observant friend had guessed most of it. The other members of Wolf Clan and Bleythin Pack who worked together thought that Joe had left San Diego and the Bleythin detective agency because he craved even more adventure in his life.

He'd actually left because he hated Sid's guts and wanted absolutely no contact with her. She didn't blame him. In fact, she'd originally offered to leave, but he wouldn't hear of it. So now she bore the extra guilt of being responsible for a werewolf leaving his pack for a lone existence.

"Life sucks," Sid muttered.

"Don't it, though?" Eden answered. "Or were you voicing vampire philosophy?"

"You have no respect for my culture," Sid said.

"Just leavening your melodrama with a bit of humor. You supernatural sorts take yourself way too seriously sometimes. Look at you, for example: clinging to a lot of outmoded customs, when you're dying to break loose and live in the twenty-first century."

"Our customs help us survive," Sid answered. "I know how that sounds, after what I did to Joe and using a sperm donor to have Charles, but I do believe that our way of life mostly makes sense. I *have* to believe that," she added desperately. She looked toward the entrance of the house. The waiting was driving her crazy. "You didn't come here to try to talk me out of tonight's ceremony, did you?"

She half hoped that was why Eden had joined her in the garden, but the mortal shook her head.

"The crèche system is one that's worked very well for your people for centuries. Do you know that in all of the generations my people have hunted yours, we've never found the hiding place of a crèche? Charles is going to be perfectly safe during a time when he's most vulnerable."

"I know." Sidonie sighed. "But still—"

"I'm here for two reasons," Eden interrupted. She pointed toward the distant glow. "First, since you're going to need something to occupy you, how would you like to join a group of us that are going up to volunteer to fight the fire tomorrow?"

"Sure, why not?" Sid answered dispiritedly. "What's your second reason?"

Eden took Sid's hand and pulled her to her feet. "It's time for the ceremony. I'm here to fetch you."

There was a ceremony for every aspect of Clan and Family life. Sid understood the importance of rites of passage, but she wished they'd just let her kiss her baby good-bye and get the inevitable over with quickly.

When she came into the Wolf Clan Citadel's central gathering room, she saw Lady Juanita's bondmate holding Charles in his arms. Charles was enthusiastically gnawing on the wrist the Prime held to his mouth.

"Chuck the Vampire needs blood other than yours, mama Wolf," Laurent said, taking Sid's other hand.

"I know that," she answered miserablely.

An altar was set up in the center of the large room. Lady Juanita, the Clan Matri, stood on one side of it. Laurent led Sid to stand on the other side. Candles lent light to the windowless space, concentrated in a golden arc around the statues of the moon goddess and leaping wolf set on the altar. Clan members and friends, all either Primes or Householders, gathered in the shadows beyond the light. Sid watched the Matri, not knowing what would happen next, since you had to be a mother before you could attend a Severing.

Ugly word, that. *Severing.*

Laurent stepped behind Sid, and her mother, Lady Antonia, and her sire, Tony Crowe, came to stand beside her. Sid assumed that Charles would be brought up to the altar, but instead, Tony and Antonia grasped her arms as Laurent's fingers settled against her temples.

I just found out I have to do this, her brother's thought came to her. *I'm sorry.*

Sorry for what?

Instead of a coherent answer, the trap closed around her. Laurent's thoughts opened her mind but the vise that closed around it was made up of the telepathic power of everyone in the room.

They were going to take her baby from her! Not just physically, but in every possible way. They were going to make her forget Charles!

Of course not. Memory remains. Lady Juanita's words came to her. *This will protect you both. You won't be apart forever.*

Sid didn't believe the Matri. She didn't care even if it *was* the truth. She fought hard with every mental trick she knew to hold on to the awareness, the love they intended to steal from her.

How can you do this? she mentally screamed. *Please don't do this!*

But there was no mercy. Nothing could stop the overwhelming combined strength of those who loved her from doing what was best for her and her child.

When the darkness swept over her, Sid almost welcomed it. Knowing she'd lost, but already not remembering what she'd been fighting for, she prayed the darkness would last forever.

Chapter Three

December 12
Present Day

Joe Bleythin had no doubt that Dee McCoy was a mortal woman, but she was like no other mortal he'd ever met. For one thing, she was a full member of the Dark Angels, which meant she was tougher than nails and able to keep up with her supernatural comrades. For another, she was a witch. This didn't mean that she was just psychic, like many other mortal beings. Oh, no—Dee performed rituals and did spells, and they really worked. Joe found that very weird.

He liked to think there were scientific explanations for what happened in the world, even his werewolf ability to shape-shift. Dee had told him that magic was a combination of chemistry, physics, and biology blended with psychic energy, but he suspected she only told him that to calm him down.

He breathed deeply now to at least appear calm as Dee finished casting a protective circle around the campsite. Everyone in the Crew was tired from a day spent firefighting, but they'd agreed to go along with this ritual because Dee claimed this was the right place and the perfect time for it. Plus, Tobias had told them that he didn't want to hear any bitching; they could get some rest when it was over.

While he waited, Joe looked at the people gathered with him around the fire and wondered if he really wanted his memories back. Maybe Dee's magic wouldn't work. If it didn't, a vampire as powerful as Tobias could probably break through the blocks Sid Wolf had put in his mind. But the last thing Joe wanted was a vampire inside his head.

He'd once been violated, psychically raped by a vampire, and for a while he'd barely been able to be around any of her kind. But if you were going to be a Dark Angel, you had to be able to work with all kinds: vamps, werefolk, selkies, sorcerers—even Jerame, and nobody was quite sure what he was. Fallen angel, maybe? Elf? Anime hero brought to life? He wasn't telling, and in the Crew it was best not to ask personal questions. They were kind of like the foreign legion that way. Tobias Strahan led, the Crew followed, and nothing but getting the job done mattered.

On their off hours they partied. Or, on nights like this, they sat around and waited while one of their number submitted to a magical cleansing.

Joe drew his knees up and propped his chin on them. He sighed loudly, which got him a look from Joaquin the werejaguar.

"Feeling silly?" the other shifter asked.

"Completely." He noticed Dee moving in a slow circle around the edges of the camp. Curls of smoke rose from the clay bowl she carried. "I hate that incense she uses."

"Take a sniff," Joaquin advised. "For once, the firesmoke in the air is doing some good. It's completely covering Dee's herbs. Are we all going to have to get naked and dance around the fire this time?"

"Since when have you ever minded getting naked?" Joe asked.

"Our neighbors might mind."

Even though there were plenty of mortal fire-fighters and volunteers camped out well back from the fire line, too, Joe was confident of their privacy.

Dee finished warding the perimeter. She spoke to Tobias, who stood guard, then she turned toward Joe. He was on his feet waiting for her, tense with expectation. Or maybe he was just sick with dread.

"Is it too late to change my mind?" Joe asked the witch.

"After Tobias has agreed to it?" She jerked a thumb over her shoulder. "Why don't you go ask him?"

She knew he wouldn't. "What do you want me to do, Dee?"

She handed him a thermos cup of steaming liquid. "Drink it all."

Joe didn't look at it. He closed his eyes and chugged it down.

It tasted like strong black coffee.

"Uh, Dee, are you sure this—"

"Oh, please," she complained. "Why does everyone think magic has to be all that woo-woo stuff?" She had a fiery temper to go with her blazing red hair and snatched the cup out of his hands.

"What do I do now?"

"That's up to you," Dee said. "Do you want to remember or don't you?"

"Yes, but—"

She walked away before Joe could finish.

He sat back down and looked at Joaquin. "Mortals are nuts, have you noticed?"

Joaquin shrugged. "They have their uses."

"I don't know," Joe said, gazing into the campfire. He waited for something magical to happen, but time passed and all he was aware of was the hot wind and scent of smoke. He sighed. "Sometimes I think we should all just stick to dealing with our own species and avoid mortals altogether."

"Vampires can't do without mortals," Joaquin reminded him.

Doing without vampires might be a good idea for werefolk, Joe thought darkly. But there was only one vampire he really felt that way about.

He was relieved that Dee's magic hadn't worked. He could honestly claim that he'd given recovering his memories a try, which ought to keep Tobias off his back about the need for every member of the Crew to be psychically whole. Joe suspected that if that *was* absolutely necessary, half of them wouldn't even be here.

"Besides, hiding from mortals won't do us any good," Joaquin went on. "There's six billion of them, and they've got spy satellites and cell phones and Wi-Fi hotspots."

"We've got all that stuff," Joe pointed out.

"And we've got telepathy and all kinds of other

psychic crap," Joaquin added. "But we're still overrun by the mortals' population advantage. There's nowhere to hide because they're everywhere. Even if we did manage to isolate ourselves, the mortals would just find a way to screw the habitat even faster than they already are."

Joe pointed his chin toward the distant fire line. "Did they do that or did we?"

"That's what we're here to find out," Joaquin answered. "If we find out that the arson is our mess, we'll take down the ones responsible."

Joe couldn't fathom why any member of the supernatural community would deliberately destroy terrain—except maybe to drive out the mortals encroaching on the wild places. But figuring out the reason for any assignment wasn't his problem. His job was to kill whoever Tobias ordered them to kill.

Joaquin stood and yawned. "Been a hard day. If we're not going to get a decent show from Dee's potion, I'm going to sack out for a while before my watch."

"Sorry for the lack of entertainment." Joe got to his feet and stretched tired muscles. "Sleep sounds like a great idea."

Chapter Four

Five Years Ago

"The Carlisles' plane is now wheels up. Rejoice." Sid glanced up at the Mexican sky from the hotel balcony before she flipped shut her cell phone and turned to Joe with a dazzling smile. "We have returned a teenage runaway to the bosom of her family. Miranda is no longer our problem."

"Hallelujah and amen," Joe answered.

He saluted his partner with his beer bottle and she raised her margarita glass in response. For a few minutes, they gazed out at the beach and ocean from their third-floor balcony. Life was good without Miranda in it.

"Technically, this was an easy job," Sid said, breaking the contented silence.

"Technically," Joe said. And they both broke out laughing.

"You know, if I believed in demons I'd say Miranda was fathered by an incubus instead of doting daddy Carlisle," Sid said when she stopped laughing.

"She certainly has the sexual appetite of a succubus," Joe said.

"At sixteen, so did I."

"Yeah, but you're a vampire. You're supposed to be insatiable."

Sid fanned her face with her hand. "Why, Mr. Bleythin, you make me blush."

He looked closely at her face, lit by the setting sun. "No, I don't."

She might not have been blushing, but he did notice that his close scrutiny caused her nipples to pucker under her thin, aqua silk tank top.

"Oh, my," Joe murmured.

Sid took another sip of her drink, then ran her tongue slowly around her lips. Joe's entire body tightened, and the air between them sizzled with mutual desire.

They were partners. This was a professional relationship. He was a werewolf. She was a vampire.

But he'd been wanting to kiss her since the day they'd met.

She stood as he came around the small table. Her arms went around him as his mouth came down on hers.

Her mouth clung to his while her words came into his mind. *Do you have any idea how jealous I was when Miranda tried to seduce you?*

You were jealous of me? Joe was full of wonder. *I go green when anyone even* looks *at you.*

His hand slipped under her shirt to cup her breasts. He had every intention of kissing his way down her long, lovely neck, all the way down to the peaks of her nipples, to worship her breasts— and that was only the beginning.

Except that out here on the balcony probably wasn't a good place to do it.

Joe swung Sid into his arms and took her inside the suite. It was only a few steps to the bedroom but Joe stood in the sitting room for a while with his eyes closed, enjoying the weight of her in his arms, the warmth of her skin against his, the feel of her gold hair against his cheek, and all the marvelous scents that were the essence of Sidonie Wolf.

Her ear was pressed against his chest.

"Listening to my heartbeat?" he asked.

She stroked his neck. "Mmmmm . . . delicious."

He carried her into the bedroom and caught his breath at the way she slid slowly down his body when he set her down. Her tongue flicked across the base of his throat.

Joe groaned. "Are you going to bite me?"

Blue eyes full of mischief and desire gazed up at him. "Do you want me to?"

Good question. *Hard* question. Joe didn't want to think right now.

"Better not," he managed, though the decision was damned hard.

"Later."

Sid took his hand and led him to the bed. He wondered if she'd heard the promise in her voice and if the word frightened and thrilled her as much as it did him.

She unbuttoned his shirt and he savored every tiny touch of her fingers slowly working down his chest.

"Fuzzy," she said after his shirt dropped to the floor.

"Werefolk," he reminded her, and held his breath at the momentary fear that she'd reject him.

Instead, she spun him around and tossed him onto the bed. "Vampire," she reminded him at this feat of strength. Then she swiftly shed her clothes and straddled his hips. "*Insatiable* is the term you used, I believe? Darlin', you have no idea . . ."

She bent down for a swift kiss while he stroked her breasts. His cock strained upward against her belly, the throbbing heat and pressure driving him crazy. His hands stayed on her breasts as she sat up and she arched her back in response.

"I've waited a long time for this," he told her as he watched the pleasure on her face, the passion in her eyes.

"We both have. Joe, I—"

Chapter Five

December 13
Present Day

The raw hunger in Sid's voice still sounded in Joe's mind as he came up out of the dream. The same raw hunger echoed in his blood and bones and skin. He reached for her, knowing he'd find nothing but empty air, knowing he was alone in the dark. The pain of the memory brought him awake with tears in his eyes.

Acrid smoke in his nostrils and stinging the back of his throat reminded him of where he was. He lay on his back in the tent and swore to himself at the realization that Dee's memory potion had worked all too well.

Joe sat up and rubbed his throbbing temples. What had Dee put in that potion of hers?

Joe noted the distinct scents of the two other Crew members inside the tent. The night scents and sounds outside were less than they should be because the animals and people had fled the area of the fire. He heard the sounds of helicopters and planes in the distance as the night shift fought the blaze. He picked out the smells of fuel and fire retardant. Wind whipped and the night roared. The situation outside wasn't pleasant, but all was as it was supposed to be.

Inside the tent people slept, and that was as it was supposed to be. Outside people passed on guard duty or sat around talking, waiting for the day.

Everyone slept but him, because he'd been woken by a nightmare. That was all it was, he told himself, just a bad dream.

A bad dream about great sex.

He wiped the sweat off his brow and tried to think of something other than his erection. Dee had used the power of suggestion to put him in a mood where he expected to remember something and that had triggered the dream and—

Except that it had all happened. Every word. Every touch. Every smell and taste and sensation.

Joe couldn't deny the reality of it for more than a few seconds.

"Goddess damn it," he muttered.

He remembered tracking the runaway Miranda Carlisle from California to a resort town on the Baja peninsula. He could remember the taste of cold beer and the sparkle of light on the water. He wanted to remember anything but the things that demanded his attention.

Damn Dee.

Damn Sidonie Wolf.

The thought of her name opened the floodgates.

"What are you staring at?" Sid asked. "Are you peering into my soul? I think I should warn you that—"

"You have the most beautiful eyes I've ever seen."

He leaned up on one elbow and stroked her blushing cheek. The long length of her warm body pressed against his in the bed, every delicious curve so right against him. They'd been resting together for a long time. Days. They'd make love, they'd sleep, they'd talk a little then they'd make love again. He was hungry, but only for her.

"Everything about you is the most beautiful I've ever seen."

She ran her fingers through his hair, pressed her palm against the back of his neck. "You shouldn't be talking like this, Joe."

"Why not?"

A sad smile played across her lips. "Because it tempts me to say similar things."

"Like what?"

She gave in to his eagerness. "Well, like how I love how black and soft your hair is. And how your voice always turns me on even when you're just saying 'Do you want another cup of coffee?' Or 'Answer the phone, will ya?'"

"Do I say will ya?"

"You do."

She ran a finger from his neck down his spine. The current from her touch sprang straight into his cock. She arched up and he moved between her legs. The next thing he knew, he was inside her again, living for her surrounding heat and their endless pleasure.

"Damn it!" Joe jumped to his feet, or would have, if he hadn't gotten tangled in the sleeping bag. He ended up rolling into one of his tent mates.

"Animal grace isn't your strong point," Dee murmured sleepily as he scrambled away from her.

"What the hell did you give me?" he demanded.

"The truth." She yawned. "Get out of here before you wake us all up."

Joe managed to step over her to the entrance without causing any more trouble. Once outside, he looked up at the smoke-obscured stars and took long, deep breaths. He managed to get his arousal under control after a few minutes, mastering the ache in his body. But the one in his heart was still killing him.

Why on earth had he thought he *wanted* to remember?

Because—

"We can't go on like this," Sid said as he came up behind her on the balcony.

Moonlight lit her pale hair and took his breath away. Joe's arms went around her waist and he leaned his cheek into the soft strands. "I know," he answered. She'd come out to the balcony while he'd been on the phone. "The folks back at the office are not happy about our taking an unscheduled Baja holiday."

She chuckled, then sighed. "How long have we been neglecting home, hearth, and duties?"

"We've been humping like bunnies for three days."

She stiffened, then turned in his arms to look at him in wide-eyed alarm.

"Don't worry," Joe said. "I didn't tell them what we've been up to."

The Bleythin detective agency was a family-run business. The last thing he and his partner needed was to return to teasing from his brothers back at the office.

"Good. Good." She gave a relieved little laugh. "We can't let anyone know about this. I can't even let anyone suspect."

That sounded far more serious than being afraid of teasing.

"Uh, hon—" he started.

Her fingertips settled on his temples. It gave him the odd image of exotic butterflies lighting on him. "This won't hurt you a bit," she said. "Forget."

Joe threw back his head and howled at the smoke-obscured stars. He was a werewolf, nobody in the camp thought this odd. He did get yelled at for disturbing peoples' rest, and a boot came sailing out of the night to hit him on the shoulder. But nobody asked what was wrong.

He couldn't have told them anyway. His insides burned with humiliation, and his heart ached too much for him to speak. He could barely form thoughts. For a long time, his only thought was, *I hate you, Sidonie Wolf.*

Chapter Six

December 14

"Thanks for helping me move my stuff back home," Sid said as she closed her town house door.

"No problem," Tony Crowe answered. "It's not like you had that much to bring back."

"True." She set down her suitcase and laptop and looked around the living room. "I've missed my place. I don't know why I let Lady Juanita talk me into being a guest at the Citadel for so long."

To protect your son. He said cheerfully, "Well, you're home now. For a couple of hours anyway."

He followed Sid into the kitchen, where she

rummaged in the freezer and brought out a bag of coffee.

"Want some?" she asked.

"Yes, please."

Tony watched her carefully for any sign of doubt, any sign of trouble.

She turned back to him when the scent of brewing coffee filled the air. "Are you sure you don't want to go firefighting with us?"

Tony shook his head. "That's not my sort of thing, sweetheart."

"You're a Clan Prime," she reminded him. She ticked off his accomplishments on her fingers. "You've been a soldier, a cop, and you now run security for every supernatural-run business in Los Angeles."

He nodded. "Yes, all very brave and heroic, but you will notice that I'm a city Prime. Fighting forest fires is so . . . rural."

"Being a soldier during World War Two wasn't?"

He chuckled. "Honey, I got to Paris as soon as I could and stayed there." More or less. Most of the time.

"Except for a cold winter trip into Belgium," she reminded him.

He stiffened "I don't want to talk about that."

"I know." She poured two cups of coffee, then they carried them outside to the tiled patio.

Painted pots of cactus circled the perimeter of the tiny fenced-in yard. Instead of grass, the yard itself was covered in a layer of decorative stones. Tony approved of the décor, and not just because it was suited to the desert environment. Anyone coming in over the fence would have to deal first with the cactus spines, then with the crunch of stones underfoot. Their kind had to think about security before beauty every time.

"It's December," Sidonie said after they sat in silence for a while.

Tony gave her a suspicious look. "Are you making a Christmas list?"

"I celebrate the Solstice, Dad," she reminded him. "You're the one who takes an interest in Christmas. The anniversary's coming up."

Tony almost groaned in frustration. His daughter might not like to think of herself as a typical vampire female, but she had matchmaking in her blood.

He sipped his coffee. "I'm not rising to your bait, sweetheart."

She was undaunted. "I was thinking that maybe you should come up to the fire line with us—to keep your mind off of it."

"My mind would not be on *it* if you weren't bringing it up."

"Bullshit."

He sighed and sat back in his chair. "Yeah, you're right. December always makes me nostalgic."

"It breaks your heart, you mean."

"There's nothing I can do about that."

Sid nodded. "The family tendency to stoicism sucks, doesn't it?" she asked bitterly.

His tone was equally so when he answered, "We serve our Clans."

She turned her chair toward his, leaned forward, and asked eagerly, "Why should you put up with it any longer? Why not dump all this Clan Prime obedience, since the Corvus Clan Matri who made that stupid decision died decades ago? Why not fly free, Crowe?"

So spoke the trapped Wolf. He didn't blame Sidonie for chafing at the bonds of duty and custom and biology, but he didn't like her urging him to do what she could not.

"Am I feeding your rebellious spirit?" she asked.

He got up and walked around the tiny yard, his footsteps crunching on the stones. "It doesn't need feeding," he said when he came back to her.

The conversation was interrupted by the sound of the doorbell. Sid went to answer it and returned with Eden and Laurent. Tony stood to greet Eden and as usual gave Laurent Wolf a long, assessing look. And as usual, Laurent smiled knowingly in response. He was nothing if not irrepressible.

After several years of knowing Laurent, Tony still reserved judgment on Sidonie's older half brother. When he'd first met him, Laurent had been firmly in the camp of the bad guys. Born and raised a Tribe Prime, he served his evil Tribe sire. Laurent had changed his ways after falling for mortal Eden and surviving some tricky machinations Sid instigated to get him away from the Dark Side.

He wasn't the first Tribe Prime to change his ways, but such Primes were usually taken in by the Families, which had lower standards of behavior than the Clans. Laurent had been accepted as a Wolf Prime by his mother Antonia's Clan. Tony liked him—it was hard not to—but trust a reformed Tribe Prime?

"You still perceive a whiff of brimstone around me, don't you, Tony?" Laurent asked him.

"Shouldn't I?" Tony asked.

"He's never going to be an angel," Eden spoke up. She put her arm around Laurent's waist. "And we wouldn't want him any other way. I've got a question for all of you," the mortal woman went on. "In what truly stupid way are mortals and immortals alike?" She didn't give them time to guess. "Because we're as likely to run toward a raging inferno as we are to run away from it. Are we all ready to go risk our lives up in the mountains?" she added.

"Not me," Tony said. He looked steadily at his daughter and responded to the hope in her eyes. "I have to go see about a girl."

Chapter Seven

December 15

"What are you thinking?" Eden asked Sid as the old bus rattled its way up the winding dirt road. The acrid smell and haze grew stronger with every upward turn.

Sid looked up and saw her sister-in-law gazing at her intently over the back of the seat in front of her. She didn't appreciate the total attention she'd been getting from everyone she encountered today.

"I'm thinking that I wish I hadn't had so much coffee before we left," she answered.

Eden nodded sympathetically. "Let's hope there are porta-potties up at the staging area."

Beside her Laurent snorted. He looked around as well. "Ah, the glamorous vampire life."

"And werefolk," Jimmy Dyami said from the seat behind her. "I don't know why I didn't fly here instead of getting my teeth rattled out on this bus."

"Because we decided to save our energy for when it's needed," his mate Alise said.

"And the usual precautions," he added with a sigh.

They were of the raptor folk, the rarest form of shape-shifter. Jimmy and Alise could turn into eagles. In human form they were short and slender, with Native American features, but they turned into the biggest damn bald eagles any mortal had ever seen. They and their other raptor kin took special care not to be sighted by mortal eyes.

Sid was surprised and proud that this rare, secretive pair was among the volunteers. Maybe it was another sign of the changes going on among the werefolk.

Stop that, she warned herself sternly. *I will not think about changes in werefolk culture. What's going on with the shape-shifters has nothing to do with me, or with vampire culture.*

There was no hope for her, and she knew it. After all this time she ought to have been used to it. She shouldn't even have been thinking about it anymore. She stared down at her clasped hands and let herself be miserable for a few minutes.

When she took a bracing breath and looked up again, she saw Laurent and Eden watching her carefully. "Stop it," she demanded. They dutifully faced forward and didn't bother her for the rest of the ride.

"... and I'd barely gotten my clothes back on before this television reporter stumbled into the woods and asked me if I'd seen a giant bird flying in the area," Jimmy told them as they got off the bus.

"And you said?" Laurent asked.

"I told her that the reason I was in the woods was that I was a cryptozoologist researcher who had been tracing the Thunderbird legend for years."

"She bought it," Alise said.

Jimmy grinned. "She interviewed me as an expert witness. I said that sadly, I'd never found any traces of the giant birds people claimed to have sighted in the area." The were-eagle sounded both disappointed and naïve, drawing a laugh from the volunteer group.

"I'm not sure if that's just mean, or absolutely brilliant," Eden said.

"Brilliant," Sid, and every other immortal within earshot, answered the mortal among them.

"Just expressing one point of view," Eden said as she stepped off the bus.

Sid pointed. "The johns are over there."

She and Eden crossed the parking area, leaving Laurent to unload their gear from the bus.

"What are you two up to?" Sid asked. "And don't try to look innocent."

"Laurent and I are frequently up to something," Eden replied. "Could you be more specific?"

"You're both treating me like I'm really fragile, and it's getting on my nerves."

"Ah, well . . ."

They'd reached the portable toilets, and Eden ducked inside. Sid looked at the closed door in annoyance, then entered the little green outhouse next door.

Eden was halfway back to the bus when Sid came back outside, but she caught up with her sister-in-law in a moment.

"Well, what?" Sid demanded.

Yet Sid knew, even as she asked the question. How could she be so close to Joe Bleythin and not know? She was aware of his vital masculine energy even before she saw the tall, black-haired figure standing by the bus. Her first impulse was to find somewhere to hide, or to run back down the mountain.

But anger took over and she turned on Eden, barely able to control the longing to spout fangs and claws and rip the mortal to shreds. "You *knew* he was here. You knew and you didn't tell me?"

Anger flashed briefly in Eden's dark eyes, and she looked like she was going to argue. "I di—" She shook her head. "Ours is a small world, Sid. You have to face him sometime."

"No, I don't! I'm a vampire, he's a werewolf. He's—"

Eden put herself between Sid and the sight of Joe. She came very close and whispered fiercely, "You made your choice. Deal with it. Right now."

Sid backed up a step. Her heart twisted and she wanted to cry, but the mortal woman stared her down. "Damn it, Eden. You are such a hardass."

Eden put her hand comfortingly on Sid's shoulder. "Somebody in this family of noble Wolf Clan wusses has to be."

Sid carefully uncurled her fists, then deliberately relaxed her tense shoulders. She ignored the anger, the regret, the fear of impending humiliation. She lifted her chin proudly. She couldn't hide behind the alpha male "I am Prime" crap, but she could wear the haughty "I am a vampire female; worship the ground I tread on, puny male" attitude. It was probably the best armor for this situation anyway.

"You're right," she told Eden. "I hate you, but you are right. It looks like our guide up to the base camp has arrived. Let's get back to our group, shall we?"

Chapter Eight

Despite the roaring fire in the distance and the organized chaos of the crowded volunteer station, Joe knew Sidonie Wolf was there. All of his senses burned with awareness of her. He was on fire, but he refused to turn around, to look for her.

Every released memory of their lovemaking raced through him and he had to work hard to remind himself that the ecstasy she'd brought him hadn't happened last night, but years ago.

Ecstasy she'd stolen from him.

"When are you coming home for a visit?" Laurent asked him.

Joe got the impression that this wasn't the first time the vampire had spoken to him.

"When are you coming back to work?" Laurent added.

Clearly, nobody at Bleythin Investigations still knew his reasons for leaving. Joe was grateful to Sid for that, for a split second at least. "That's not happening," he told Laurent.

Laurent frowned. "From your cold tone, I take it that I should back off and ask about the weather or something."

Joe nodded. "Yeah, that would work. The weather, by the way, is hot and smoky."

He barely got the words out before Sid's entrancing scent cut through his senses. She was coming closer.

The realization nearly dragged him to his knees, nearly pulled him around with the longing to see her.

Joe forcibly reminded himself of what she'd done and managed to stay perfectly still as she passed by. She didn't acknowledge him but moved to stand at the back of the volunteer group. He managed not to sneer at her or to snarl that he was surprised the Clan had allowed their princess out of the tower.

Eden gave him a nod as she came up to join Laurent. As the Prime put his arm around his wife's shoulder, their closeness tore at Joe. There were other mated pairs among this group, and he hated the reminder that he was packless. For a moment he hated them all.

Except he wasn't alone. He was a Dark Angel. He was one of the Crew, and that was enough. He couldn't walk away from this group even if Sid *was* here. He had orders from Tobias.

He gestured for the group to follow him farther away from any mortal ears, waiting to speak until they were completely alone.

"Listen up, persons of the furred, fanged, and feathered persuasion," he called.

Laughter rose, but he noticed that Sid wasn't among the ones who looked amused.

"You volunteered to help fight the fire, but that's not the real reason you are here. There are plenty of mortals for that job."

People exchanged questioning looks.

"You are here to help the Dark Angels do the work that's necessary for our survival."

"We get to kick some ass?" Rayhan, a Wolf Clan Prime, asked.

"You wish," Joe answered. "We may get to do that eventually, but first we are going to find, analyze, and then destroy any evidence that the fires were set by rogue immortals."

"Rogue?" someone asked.

"The Angels suspect *us* of arson?" someone else asked angrily. "That's ridiculous!"

"That's a typical Clan reaction," Laurent put in. "You people don't know how to think like the bad guys."

"Because we weren't born Tribe," Rayhan sneered at him.

"Tobias Strahan of Family Singan was born Tribe," Joe pointed out to the vampires. "We Angels follow him without question."

"So there," Eden said teasingly, and stuck out her tongue.

The mortal woman's sarcasm cut the tension between the Primes. Living among the discipline and camaraderie of the Crew, Joe had almost forgotten how touchy relations between various types of immortals could be.

"No one suspects *you* of anything," Joe went on. "But there have been problems in the last few years—"

"Tribe vampires selling knock-off daylight drugs that we haven't been able to trace to the source," Eden interjected. "Neo-Nazi werewolves, with a huge budget we also haven't been able to trace, trying to start a revolution against the immortal councils. Mortals doing scientific experiments on kidnapped vampires to find the secrets of eternal youth. Fanatical vampire hunters claiming they have scientists working on ways to destroy immortals. We don't know if any of it is linked, or if there's more going on behind the plots we managed to stop—but paranoia doesn't hurt when you want to live a quiet life."

Joe was almost relieved that Eden had brought all this up. Everyone was aware that she'd been born into the Faveau family of vampire hunters, a group of mortals who now worked with vampires to keep bad guys from exploiting both sides of the mortal/immortal world. Eden *knew* stuff. She was trusted.

Joe said, "In your day jobs, some of you are cops and detectives and forensic scientists. We need that expertise, along with your psychic senses, to find the cause of this devastation before the mortals have time to investigate."

"That sounds like a good idea," Rayhan Wolf conceded. "We do have talents you military muscle types don't have."

Joe let it go. "That's why you are going to be divided up to work with three Dark Angels teams to do a grid search of the fire area."

Joe paused a moment for dramatic effect, then added, "Everyone except you, Sidonie. You can't possibly be exposed to danger."

He expected an explosion and relished the thought of her furious and thwarted. Her eyes blazed red for a moment, and he awaited the lecture about how she was as strong and as fast and as capable as any male vampire in the bunch.

Instead her expression went cold. She looked at him like he was a bug and he thought his blood was going to freeze.

She asked, "What am I supposed to do?"

The last thing he'd expected was cooperation. It took Joe a moment to answer, "You can make sure everyone's packs get transported up to the Angels camp. I'll assign a couple of my people to help you."

"Fine." Sid turned away from him.

He was dismissed, forgotten.

Feeling like he was recovering from a body blow, Joe began to issue commands to the rest of the group.

Chapter Nine

"You can't possibly be exposed to danger," Sid mocked. "He said oh so solicitously. Oooh, Joe thinks he's so clever. When I think of the danger we used to get into together, I could just—oohhh!"

She tossed a backpack into the supply tent and turned around as Eden tossed her another one from the trailer hitched to the ATV. She'd been seething the whole way up the canyon to the campsite but had waited until she and her friend were alone before saying anything.

"I thought you handled it very well," Eden answered. "Your response was very mature, if a bit bitchy."

"Bitchy? *Joe's* the one who—"

"Abused his power back there? Yes, he did." Eden jumped down off the trailer and gave Sid a hard look. "But now that you've both counted coup, you are both going to act in a mature, civilized manner for the duration of the emergency. Aren't you?"

Sid gritted her teeth, and her fangs bit into her lower lip. "You didn't come along to help with the luggage," she accused the mortal. "You came along to give me that lecture."

"Yep. And I'll slap Joe upside the head the first chance I get, too."

Sidonie began to laugh. The pain in her heart and her gut wasn't any better, but her head cleared somewhat.

"You're right about my having to live with what I did, and without Joe. But damn it, how do you expect me to defend myself from how I feel?"

"Find a nice vampire boy to fall in love with."

"Do you think I haven't tried?"

"Not hard enough."

Eden's practicality made Sid want to throw things. "How does my brother put up with you?"

"He likes 'em mean and bossy."

Laurent had all the dominant alpha tendencies of any Prime, along with having survived to adulthood in Tribe Manticore. Sid had had a small taste of how rough life in the Tribes could be and knew her brother was anything but soft.

"He likes *you* mean and bossy," Sid said.

"That's good—because it's too late for me to change now."

Sid knew that she was the one who needed to change. She'd been trying unsuccessfully since the day she realized she was much too attracted to Joe Bleythin.

She sighed. "Maybe looking for a nice vampire boy to fall in love with has been the wrong strategy. Maybe I need somebody tough and hard and ruthless to get me interested in Primes."

"Maybe you do."

"But where do I look, when just about every Prime in the Clans has tried their hand at courting me?"

"Um . . ." Eden was looking past Sid's shoulder, her eyes wide. She pointed. "How about him?"

Sid turned to look at the Prime standing in front of a tent on the other side of the camp. "Oh, my goddess . . ." she whispered.

"If I wasn't already happily married . . ." Eden said.

"Is that the legendary Tobias?" Sid asked.

"He wouldn't dare be anybody else."

The object of their attention was broad shouldered, six foot six, with thick auburn hair, sharp cheekbones, a square chin, and huge brown eyes. There had to be the body of a god underneath the loose-fitting camos he was wearing.

"Well, isn't he just the Prime's Prime," Eden said, returning to her less-than-impressed-with-the-whole-vampire-mystique, sarcastic self.

Sid dragged her gaze away from him. "Yes, indeed," she said with a smile.

"Go. Introduce yourself. Have your way with him. Let me know all the details."

Sid snorted. "You know that's not how it works. The Prime always approaches the female."

"Why?" Eden put her hands on her hips. "Because it's always been done that way? I thought you were all about changing female roles in vampire culture."

"I am. Eventually. When I can."

"You've already done more than any other vampgirl to win your freedom."

But at what cost? More than Sid could bear to think about most of the time. "I have to be careful."

"You've spent the last two years being a bit too careful, haven't you? Of course you've had Charles to look after, but—" Eden looked at her worriedly. "You are okay about Charles, aren't you?"

Her son was in perfectly good hands. He was

where he needed to be. The Clan was doing what was best for him to grow up into a proper, socialized Prime.

"Of course I am," she answered her sister-in-law. "I'm actually looking forward to having time for myself again."

"Good." Eden jerked her head toward the big Prime across the way. "Then I say go for it."

Sid looked back at the legendary Tobias. He was talking to a red-haired mortal woman. Sid wasn't going to disturb him while he was busy.

"He's not bonded, is he?" Eden asked after watching the pair for a few moments. Eden was very smart and incredibly observant, but Sid knew she didn't have a molecule of psychic talent. On the other hand, Sid was extremely psychically gifted.

She closed her eyes and concentrated to get a feel for the energy around her. Sharp pain shot through her head, followed by a split second of nausea. She opened her eyes to discover that she was sitting on the ground with Eden standing worriedly over her.

"What happened?" Sid asked, dazed.

"I was going to ask *you*."

"It felt like I hit a mental wall." Sid took deep breaths.

"Do you think the Dark Angels have some kind of mental barrier up?"

"Probably, but we're inside the perimeter. I think mommy duty has put me out of practice for dealing with the grown-ups."

Eden gave a thoughtful nod. "Yeah. That's probably it."

Sid rubbed her temples. "I feel bruised. Let me try again."

She closed her eyes once more. This time she ignored the pain, and it soon settled down to a faint headache she had no trouble ignoring as she studied the local flow of energy.

"I don't detect bond energy from anybody but you," Sid told Eden when she opened her eyes.

"So the big boy's not taken."

"But there are a lot of people with crushes on him," Sid added. "The hero worship permeating this place is nauseating."

"You're just trying to find an excuse not to like him, like you do with every Prime you meet. Go."

Sid got to her feet. "I am getting tired of this need you have to be honest with me today."

Eden crossed her arms. "You know how to make me back off."

Sid held her hands up in surrender. "I'm going, I'm going."

She turned around and walked over to introduce herself to the glorious man-mountain that was Tobias Strahan.

"Welcome, Lady Sidonie," he said as she came near. He had a deep, delicious voice. "You're the one that I want."

Before she could respond, he put his arm around her shoulders and led her into his tent.

Chapter Ten

Joe felt like he was going to smell of smoke for the rest of his life. He gratefully took the bucket of water Dee offered him and poured it over his head. Soot and sweat sluiced off him as the water poured through his hair and down his bare chest.

"Thanks. That felt good," he said as he handed the bucket back.

Dee looked him over. "Looks good, too. Too bad your girlfriend's not around to get a look at your water-slicked six-pack," she added.

"Where is Sid?" The words came out before he could stop them. He glared at Dee. "Stop pulling witchy stuff on me."

"Think what you like," she said.

"You didn't answer my question," he called after her.

She turned a mischievous grin on him. "She's with Tobias. They've been in his tent for hours." She took her bucket and walked away, hooting with laughter.

As Joe stared after the witch, Laurent came up and put his hand on his shoulder. "Did I overhear something about Sid?"

Joe ground his teeth together to keep from snapping. "Sid, Sid, Sid," he muttered. "It's a stupid name for a woman anyway."

"She's not a woman," Laurent reminded him. "She's a vampire female. You have to admit that Sidonie the vampire sounds much classier than Chuck the vampire."

Joe turned an angry look on Laurent. "Who the hell is Chuck?"

"Her kid."

The news hit Joe hard in the gut. He spun around to face Tobias's tent. "She had a . . ."

"I thought you knew she had a baby." Laurent stepped back and gave Joe an odd look. "Don't you special ops types get e-mail from home? Or didn't your brothers mention all the changes back at the office since you left?"

"Sid had a baby? She's bonded?" Joe's throat tightened on the word. His heart raced.

"Who said anything about her having a bond-mate? She did her duty by the Clan, and then gave my nephew the dullest, most weenie name any Prime is ever going to have to live down. I'm surprised Sid didn't tell you about Chuck, since she's always claimed you're her best friend. Are you okay, Joe? You look a little green."

She had a child. Maybe she wasn't bonded, but she'd had a relationship with someone. With another vampire, of course, with one of her own kind. He'd never meant anything more to her than a fling, a few days of slumming with a lesser species.

"Friend?" Joe laughed. "We were a little bit more than friends."

"Right, you were partners, but you're the one who left to join up with this macho bunch." Laurent looked around almost furtively. "Have you noticed that even the girls around here are macho?"

"You have to be tough to be in the Crew."

Laurent gave a mock shudder. "Eden loves it here. I hope she doesn't try to get me to join up. I've come to love the comforts of home and hearth."

"You're chattering," Joe told Laurent. "You do that when you're trying to cover up something."

Laurent glanced toward Tobias's tent. "I'll admit it, I'm worried about my sister. Funny thing is, a few years ago I didn't want anything to do with family. Now I worry about them all the time—my wife, my kid, my nephew, my mom, especially my sister."

Despite not wanting anything to do with Sid, Joe couldn't stop the question. "Why your sister?"

"Because—Well, what have we here?" Laurent asked as Sid and Tobias came out of the tent. Tobias's arm was snugly around her shoulder.

"Maybe they've been bonding," Joe said.

"You sound jealous," Laurent responded. "Don't tell me you're interested in my sister. Is that why you left?"

"It's none of your business."

That didn't deter Laurent. "If you're in love with her it's a good thing you left, because I can't think of a quicker way for you to get yourself killed."

"I am not impressed by your brotherly concern."

"That's not—"

Before Laurent could finish, two trucks came rumbling to a halt just below the campsite. Six uniformed men got out and headed uphill.

"Mortals," Joe and Laurent said together.

Everyone else in the camp noticed as well, and most people began to head toward the intruders.

Tobias lifted a hand and called, "Stand down."

The Crew waited, and made sure their guests did as well, while Tobias went down the hill to greet the military. He took Sid with him.

Joe waited with equal parts surprise and annoyance while the two vampires talked to the intruders. The newcomers were tense and not at all friendly. At one point, Sid moved away from Tobias. She reached out to gently touch the commander on the arm. In a moment she had the mortal's complete attention.

Joe's breath hissed out as he took a step forward. Laurent put an arm out to hold him back, and fury flashed through Joe at himself for reacting after Tobias had given the command to stay put, and for having to be reminded of it by an outsider.

"She's good," Laurent murmured.

The mortal commander was looking into Sid's eyes, his expression blank. It was easy to see that Sidonie was pulling her mind-muddling telepathic trick on the unsuspecting mortal. She was no doubt telling him that Tobias's group was an official part of the firefighting contingent, telling him that he had more important things to do than interfere with the work of people who had every right and good reason to be there.

When mortals had stopped by before, Tobias had made them believe this, and Joe had been as amused as every other member of the Crew. Now that Tobias had put Sid to work doing what she did best—lying to people and making them believe it—Joe didn't see any humor in it at all.

Chapter Eleven

Sid waited with the Dark Angel commander as he watched the National Guard contingent get back in their trucks and drive away. She felt the psychic weight of every eye on her from the camp behind them. The attention didn't help her headache any, and it certainly didn't help the feeling of being disgusted with herself.

If she didn't know Joe was watching, she might have been basking in smug satisfaction at a job well done. Allaying mortal suspicions about the supernatural world was necessary at times. You didn't alter peoples' thoughts for fun, but for the safety of everyone involved.

Joe knew that.

But that wasn't what he was thinking right now, was it? She knew Joseph Bleythin. He was somehow remembering what she'd done to him and hating her more by the second for it.

Maybe he was right, too.

"Screw him anyway," she muttered.

Tobias cocked one finely arched brow at her, then walked back to the camp.

As Sid followed, Eden gestured for her to come into the supply tent.

"What did Tobias want?" Eden asked as soon as they were alone. "Did he try to seduce you or recruit you?"

Sid laughed. "Since when would a Prime even think about letting a vampire female join a club like the Dark Angels?"

"Things have to change sometime."

"I doubt if it'll be in this lifetime."

She couldn't share the mortal's attitude, not from where she stood inside the luxurious cage of a female vampire's life. She hoped to have daughters and to work to get them the freedom she'd never fully have herself.

"So he wanted to seduce you."

Sid laughed again. "Primes try to do that automatically."

Eden grinned. "Is he as talented as he is lovely?"

Sid shrugged. "I wouldn't know. We had a nice flirt, but what he really wanted was to talk. Speaking of talking," she went on before Eden asked any more questions, "did you get your chance to smack Joe upside the head? Have we both promised to behave now?"

"I sent Laurent to talk to him," Eden answered. "The hope is that a talk between guys would work better than my nagging him."

"You nagged me."

"Males have more delicate sensibilities." Eden was not to be diverted. "What did Tobias want to talk about?"

"Nothing significant. He takes a morbid interest in the time I spent with Tribe Manticore. I told him that I was locked in a room the whole time I was their prisoner. I have no information about Dawn production or distribution routes or secret labs. You probably know more than I do."

"Nah," Eden answered. "The Dawn junkies I interrogated didn't know or care where the stuff came from. And the Dark Angels have access to the report I put together."

"Tobias mentioned that."

Just then, Dee stuck her head into the tent. "Outside, you two. Tobias has called dinner, with a meeting after."

"Lordy, but they do love to jump to his tune,"

Eden said when Dee was gone. She lifted the tent flap and gestured Sid out. "Shall we?"

"At least we get a meal to go along with tonight's scheduled lecture," Laurent whispered in Sid's ear as she took a seat beside him. "I was scared we'd have to live off the land. Not that I couldn't kill a bear to feed my woman," he added staunchly, with a glance toward Eden.

Eden looked up from her seat opposite Laurent at the long mess table. "I'm sure you could kill a bear, dear. Of course, then you'd wait for a gourmet chef to come along and do something with it while you studied the wine list."

"Of course I would. Darling. I started life as a monster, not as a barbarian."

Sid smiled as she watched Laurent flutter his impossibly long eyelashes at his bondmate. Eden covered her mouth to hide a giggle.

The other volunteers were scattered among the serious ranks of the Dark Angels, and silence was the order of the day as they quickly ate their dinner. Sid couldn't detect much telepathic activity, either. After all, Tobias had called a meeting; they had to get through the mundane stuff quickly so they could give their complete attention to the boss.

Sid noticed that Joe had sat as far away from her as he could get. After one glance, she deliberately didn't look his way. She told herself she imagined feeling his gaze on her.

"You two better behave," she whispered to Eden and Laurent. "Or you'll end up doing five thousand push-ups for enjoying yourself."

Eden composed her features and said seriously, "I admire the strength of character required to lead a disciplined life like this. Special Ops teams are necessary. That doesn't mean I want us to sign up," she added to Laurent before he had the chance to look horrified.

Laurent looked to the opposite end of the table. "I wouldn't have thought this would be Joe's sort of lifestyle."

"He used to be in the air force," Sid said. "He always talked about going back to the military when things at work got hairy."

She closed her lips tightly, surprised at how she'd automatically jumped to Joe's defense. Well, why not? She didn't really have any reason to be angry at him. At least, she didn't have any right to be.

"He was a werewolf working with werewolves," Laurent pointed out. "Things were always hairy."

He shouldn't have left his pack, Sid thought.

He probably just wanted another way to make me feel guilty.

Good goddess, she was pouting again! She didn't understand why being near Joe was making her emotions as volatile and angsty as a teenage mortal's. Hormones, maybe? Every fiber of her being currently burned with lust, but none of the virile Primes among the Angels and volunteers did anything for her.

Sid couldn't stop a second glance toward Joe. And this time their gazes met.

"I've never seen eyes as blue as yours."

"I probably have some husky in my background," Joe answered.

Sid couldn't laugh. She couldn't even smile. All she could do was to continue to stare deep into Joe's eyes as he stared into hers. Their souls met. And their flesh—

His fingers slid over her bare skin as softly as the tropical moonlight that poured down onto the balcony. The tang of sea salt met her already heightened senses when she licked her lips. Her fingers traced across his body, reveled in the feel of well-defined, hard muscles. The air heated between them and—

"Contrary to popular belief, vampires really do need oxygen." Eden's voice assaulted Sid's ears.

There was no salt in the air, no moonlight.

Only the faint tang of smoke when she took in a sharp breath.

From then on, she concentrated on finishing her meal.

She wasn't going to look at Joe again. She wasn't, she wasn't, she wasn't.

Chapter Twelve

"All right, people, here's what we've got so far," Tobias said.

The dishes were cleared away, and Tobias stood at the head of the table for the briefing. Joe still fought off the arousal contact with Sid had stirred in him a half hour before. He tried to keep his attention on his commander, but visions of Sid's naked body danced through his head and straight to his groin.

Sitting beside him, Dee brushed her thigh against his and said, "Just take deep breaths."

"Stop it," Joe growled. "You're not helping."

"I am," she whispered.

He finally realized that her touch was relaxing, not arousing. "Thanks."

Tobias gave him a stern look that blew away every last shred of Joe's distraction before returning his attention to the general populace.

"Our search has come up with eight separate arson sites. Eight, people. This was a vicious, systematic, and well-planned attack. Somebody was attempting to burn down California, and we've determined that that somebody swims in our side of the genetic pool."

Tobias put his hands on his hips and waited.

Surprisingly, none of the volunteers made any knee-jerk protests about the harmless intentions of the supernatural community. Joe figured they were either too intimidated by Tobias, or they'd found the evidence that the Crew had left for them to stumble on to too compelling to ignore.

The point of this exercise *was* to send them home to rally support for the coming war. The evidence was real. And these witnesses were credible, respected members of their kinds, not as easy for the elders to dismiss as a bunch of gung-ho militaristic hotheads.

Tobias continued, "It was an attack on the mortals' environment, it was an attack on the mortals' economy, and there have been five reported deaths, as well as many injuries. While I personally don't care much about mortals, we do have to live secretly among them.

"The Dark Angels have always taken on renegades, but the danger is different now. The evidence found here shows a wider conspiracy. We have found the scents of vampires, mortals, and werefolk around the eight buildings where the fires were set. Six of those buildings have left traces that tell us they were used as drug manufacturing facilities."

"Dawn labs?" Eden asked.

Tobias nodded. "Dawn was manufactured in one of the buildings. The other chemical traces we've found are still unknown. Some buildings were used for storage and as barracks. And there's a possibility that prisoners were kept in one of the buildings. The remains of a burned body were found in what might have been a cell, but that requires further investigation."

Laurent spoke up. "The layout reminded me of the werewolf base we busted a while back. Only a lot bigger."

"That lot wasn't manufacturing drugs," Rayhan Wolf said. "But Laurent's right about the similarities."

"I've seen the werewolf camp you took out in the northwest," Tobias said. "It looks like the same people financed this operation. But this time the bad guys weren't just werefolk, and they weren't busted. They finished whatever they were doing here. When they moved their operation, they set the fires to destroy evidence. The fire did its job: not even our best noses can pick up a trail among all that devastation."

"What do we do now?" Jimmy asked.

At a nod from Tobias, Dee stood up and faced the gathering. "Even we can't disguise the evidence of arson from mortal investigators. What we have to do is find out as much as we can before we turn the sites over to mortals. We'll take away our evidence, then plant evidence to direct their attention into conclusions that make sense to them.

"Methamphetamine is dangerous to produce, as well as highly illegal. We need to make it look like the fires were started by the accidental explosion of a meth lab, and that the drug-dealing mortals covered their tracks by starting all the other fires."

"None of this is too far from the truth," Tobias said. "I see nothing wrong with blackening the reputations of mortal drug traffickers while we deal with the immortal ones."

"How do we deal with them when we can't trace them?" Rayhan wanted to know.

"There are leads we're working on." Tobias

gave a brisk nod. "Divide them up into specialist teams, Dee," he told the witch.

"Yes, sir."

"Bleythin."

Joe jumped to attention. "Sir."

"Come with me."

Joe's surprise turned to dread when Tobias added, "Please come with me as well, Lady Sidonie."

Chapter Thirteen

Oh, crap, now what? Sid thought angrily.

What was she supposed to do now? The Prime had made a perfectly reasonable request and she couldn't just scream like a girl and run away because Joe was involved. He wasn't going to like this any more than she was, which was no consolation.

She gave her brother and Eden a desperate look, but their attention was concentrated on each other.

"True love sucks," Sid muttered, and forced her body into motion.

Joe walked ahead of her toward Tobias's tent,

and she found herself falling back into an old pattern: appreciating the way his long, lean body moved, the way he looked, the way he *was,* while he wasn't looking. The years she'd spent not acting on her attraction to the werewolf had honed her secret-admiration skills to a fine art—which she apparently hadn't forgotten.

It occurred to her that despite their time apart, despite her protestations to the contrary, she really hadn't tried to change.

She *couldn't* go inside the tent with Joe. The space was too small! The—

Sid took a deep breath. Panic did not become her. She lifted her chin and walked proudly past Joe when he held the tent flap open for her. Though she was careful not to brush against him, awareness of his body heat sent a damnable shiver through her.

Once inside, she went to the seat across from Tobias where she'd spent much of the afternoon, and put her attention firmly on the Dark Angels' leader. Joe remained by the entrance, and she wondered if he wanted to bolt as much as she did.

Tobias sat behind his small worktable and folded his hands on top of his closed laptop. "Lady Sidonie—"

"Sid," she corrected him, not for the first time.

"I don't require formality from a fellow vampire."

Tobias's beautiful lips thinned in irritation. He obviously wasn't used to being interrupted, or corrected. "Lady Sidonie," he went on as if she'd never spoken.

Sid was too aware of Joe's disapproving gaze on her not to let it go this time. She needed to get this over with and get out of there. She forced a polite smile and attentive attitude.

Once Tobias had her attention, he ignored her and looked at Joe. "This afternoon, Lady Sidonie and I had a discussion about her involvement with Tribe Manticore."

"Hey!" she protested. "Leave him out of this. He wasn't involved in what you want to know about."

"You were present during Lady Sidonie's extraction from the Manticore lair." Tobias continued to Joe.

"Lair?" Sid questioned.

"I was in on the rescue, yeah," Joe told his boss.

Sid sighed. She did not want to go over this again. The Manticores were not a favorite subject for any member of her immediate family.

"I remember it well. It was a very dramatic evening," she said "With lots of heroics. I've already briefed you on everything that occurred at the time. You don't need me here for Bleythin to tell you about his part in the action."

The memory of a magnificent black wolf bursting through the window of the Manticores' lair flashed across Sid's mind and she could barely stop herself from turning a dreamy smile on Joe.

"Bleythin's part in the action isn't relevant."

"It was relevant to me," she snapped. "He helped save my ass. And Eden's. And my brother's."

The faintest of smiles played around Tobias's lips. "All right. Let's say that the action that resulted in your release from the Manticores is not relevant to our current needs."

Joe stepped forward. "Current needs, sir?"

"We've gone round and round on this already," Sid told Tobias.

"But not to my satisfaction."

Frustration drove her to her feet. She accidentally bumped into Joe, and he automatically reached out to steady her.

The universe froze, if for no more than an instant.

Joe swore and backed away from her.

Sid was shaken to the core and she turned her fiery reaction on Tobias. "Your satisfaction is not my problem! We've been over and over this and I've cooperated as much as I'm going to. I don't care if you don't believe me. I'm done here."

She turned to leave, but Joe blocked the entrance. His face was hard, his body set for a fight. "What aren't you telling Tobias?" he demanded.

"Go ahead, take his side," she complained.

And good, goddess, why was she acting like a pouting teenager around Joe? It seemed like nothing in this situation with him brought out the best in her.

She suffered letting Joe take her by the shoulders and turning her to face Tobias. "Tell him what he wants to know."

Sid shivered when his breath brushed across her ear. "I don't know anything more than I've already told him—you," she added to Tobias.

The big Prime looked at her steadily, unblinking, still as stone. Michelangelo would have been proud to have done the carving. "I believe you" he finally said. "As far as it goes."

"What does that mean?" She asked Tobias.

She really wished Joe would take his hands off her. Not really. But she *needed* Joe to stop touching her before she went up in flames.

"I mean that you do not consciously remember everything you witnessed while a captive of the Manticores."

"Yes, I do."

He gave the faintest shake of his head. "There must have been conversations involving Dawn trafficking in distant rooms. There must have been stray thoughts from your captors that you didn't notice seeping into your mind. Your senses are sharp and highly concentrated, whether you're consciously using them or not. During your captivity, you were focused on staying alive and on finding a way out of a bad situation. Your senses were on full alert whether you realized it or not."

"Don't tell me what I was or wasn't doing. You weren't there."

"As I have pointed out to you before." He stood. "I need information you don't know you have."

"You're crazy." She glanced over her shoulder at Joe. "He's crazy, you know. I don't know why you follow him."

"But he does follow me, Lady Sidonie. Despite the tension between the two of you he will do as I tell him now."

She supposed the strain was evident whether or not Joe had mentioned anything about their past to his comrades.

"Just what do you want Joe to do?" she demanded.

Tobias didn't speak to her, but to Joe. "Take

her back to the places where it happened. Help her remember. Stay with her until she does."

"Hell, no!" Sid shouted.

"Yes, sir," Joe said.

Sid jerked away from Joe's hands and rounded on him. She opened her mouth to yell at him, but decided arguing wasn't going to accomplish anything. "Get out of my way," she said instead.

Joe waited, looking past her shoulder, not stepping aside until Tobias must have given a nod of permission.

Sid managed not to say *good boy* to Joe as she passed him on the way out, but she was afraid the thought escaped into the silence anyway.

Chapter Fourteen

It was actually a lovely night for a walk, Sid decided. The devastation underfoot might bring up the reek of ash with every footstep, but the burned-out undergrowth made it easier to move down the mountainside. Every now and then she'd feel heat from a still warm patch of charred ground beneath the thick soles of her athletic shoes. Maybe she should have worn hiking boots. Maybe she should have waited until morning before leaving the Dark Angels' camp, but she'd been too restless, too furious, all right—too scared—to stay.

It was a long walk home, but better that than putting up with Tobias Strahan's stupid ideas and

Joe Bleythin's accusing vibes. And the temptation he still posed for her. It was better for him that she was gone.

Maybe he's seeing that witch chick. No, probably not. He never really approved of his brother Harry marrying a mortal. Well, I'm sure there are female werefolk among the ranks of the immortal commandoes.

Sid ground her teeth, not sure whether she was more jealous of a female werewolf living a full, dangerous, active life, or of said theoretical female mating with *her* Joe.

"Both," she muttered, and kept on walking.

The crunching of the burned ground underfoot didn't disguise the sound of a vehicle coming up from behind her a few minutes later.

She should have known it wasn't going to be that easy to get away. No one had tried to stop her when she'd picked up her pack and walked away from the campsite. She'd wondered about that, but since the guard merely nodded when she saw her, Sid had kept going.

As the sound got closer and awareness kicked in from all her senses, Sid briefly considered sprinting off at an angle from the rutted dirt road to avoid a confrontation. She resisted the urge and waited with her arms crossed for the vehicle to pull to a stop beside her.

"Joseph Bleythin, I do not need or want your company," she said when he leaned out the window.

"Nor do I want yours," Joe answered.

She managed a fierce smile. "Then we agree on something."

"Get in."

The total lack of expression in his voice was really irritating. She almost asked him if the Dark Angels had stolen his soul. But she knew he would answer that *she* was the only one who'd stolen anything from him, and their descent into petty bickering would just be stupid.

"I'm going home," she said.

"You shouldn't be out here alone."

She laughed. "I'm a vampire."

"I have my orders. *Lady* Sidonie."

At least a half dozen snide remarks flashed through Sid's mind.

"You're biting your tongue," Joe said. "I can smell the blood."

Sid went around to the passenger side and got in, settling her pack on the floor beside her.

"Fasten your seat belt," Joe said, and waited until she complied before he continued the slow, bumpy ride.

"It would have been easier to walk," Sid commented after a while.

"It's a good thing you don't get car sick,"

Joe answered. "Damn!" he growled under his breath.

"It's all right," she assured him when she realized he was annoyed with himself for responding to a normal conversational comment with a normal reply. "We've spent a lot of time together. Old habits are easy to fall into. I'll take it as a given that you hate my guts, and ignore your talking to me if you'd like."

"Don't patronize me."

"I can do that, too."

She reached into her pack and pulled out her small e-reader. The backlit screen of the digital device was nice but not necessary for her vision, so she kept it on the dimmest setting. She loved the storage capacity of the little device and took it with her everywhere.

"Drive on, Jeeves," she told him. "I have something else I can do."

It didn't take long before he said exactly what she knew he would. "Whatcha reading?"

She'd always brought books on stakeouts. They'd spent many an evening sitting in the dark with her reading a paperback, frequently reading out loud to stave off boredom if Joe was interested. When they'd needed to keep quiet, she'd read to him telepathically. It had been something they'd both enjoyed.

"A vampire novel," she replied.

Sid couldn't keep from smiling as she waited for an indignant response, though it was several minutes coming. He turned the truck from the bumpy track onto a gravel road before he finally spoke.

"Why would *you* want to read a vampire novel?" Joe demanded.

"Because it was written by a vampire."

"You're kidding."

"Not at all. The general consensus is that the anonymous author is from our culture, as the hero is a Prime. It's available from an electronic publisher, for a select readership," she added. "We're calling it the Vampire Book Club."

"I bet you're also trying to keep the Matri from finding out about a book with Primes in it. They wouldn't allow anything real to get out where mortals could find it."

Sid regretted telling Joe anything about the Vampire Book Club. It was too easy to share the secret rebellions of the younger Clan females with him. That habit could prove dangerous now that he was with the Dark Angels, militant protectors of the immortal world. They might as easily go after a harmless form of entertainment as a cadre of vampire terrorists, all in the name of keeping immortals safe.

"There's nothing really real in this book," she assured Joe. "It takes place in a space empire hundreds of years in the future."

Joe showed no more interest, so Sid settled down to read while he drove from rugged mountainside to suburban foothills and on toward the city. She didn't pay attention to the outside world until she could sense more sea salt in the air than smoke.

"It's good to be home," she said.

"You haven't been gone very long," Joe said. He glanced her way. "Missing little Chuckie?"

It took her a moment to realize who he meant. "You've been talking to my brother, haven't you? My son is named Charles."

"And you're anxious to get home to your baby boy."

"Of course I—"

Sid stared straight ahead and the lights of oncoming traffic swirled and blurred around her while her mind went totally blank.

"Sid? Are you all right?"

"How odd," she murmured.

"What's wrong?"

All the blank neutrality had left his voice. He sounded like her Joe again. That was nice.

"Sidonie?"

"Charles is old enough to be in the Clan crèche now. He's safe there. I'll see him when the time is right." She smiled as the words cleared the fog from her mind. She recognized the streets now. "We're almost home."

Chapter Fifteen

"Well, good night. Thanks for the lift. Have a nice drive back." Sid got out of the truck and closed the door with a solid thump.

Joe shut off the engine and did the same.

She glared at him across the wide hood of the truck. "Ta-ta, toodleoo. Go away."

"Not happening." Joe glanced toward her front door. "We might as well go inside."

"You are not coming in my house."

"I promise not to shed on the furniture."

"I've heard that before, Joseph Bleythin."

"I wasn't feeling well that time."

"You're not well now. You've been brainwashed—by this Tobias person, not me, so don't start."

He looked around. "It's late at night in a quiet neighborhood. You don't want to start a scene."

She closed her eyes. She looked weary, and for a moment he felt sorry for her. He still wasn't leaving, though.

"I don't want to be here any more than you want me here, but we both have to live with it."

Sid shook her head and patted the hood. "This is a nice truck. I hope you enjoy sleeping in it."

Then she moved to her front door at vampire speed. She had the door open, closed, and locked behind her before Joe could take more than a few steps. He considered banging on the door or even breaking a window, but that would only cause a stir. A quiet life was a safe life. He backed away from her town house.

It wasn't as if he didn't know another way inside.

Sid barely had time to drop her pack, pour iced tea, and go out to the patio before the supernatural stirring began on the other side of the back fence. Familiar energy swirled around her and brought a fond smile, even while she wished Joe wasn't so bloody predictable.

A pack came over the top and landed on the rocks beyond the patio. A magnificent huge black wolf sprang after the pack a second later.

Sid crossed her legs. "Darn, I was hoping you'd land in the cactus. They've grown quite a bit since the last time you were here."

The wolf snatched up the pack and disappeared into the deepest shadows at the corner of the yard. Sid allowed Joe his modesty and looked at her shoes while he transformed and put his clothes back on. The temptation to look was strong, but she didn't look up until she heard the crunch of footsteps coming toward her.

Joe walked to the edge of the patio. "I figured the growth rate of your plants into my jump calculations."

"You were lucky, you mean." Sid gestured toward the second chair and the other glass of iced tea on the table.

Joe took the seat and a long gulp of the cold liquid. "You could have just let me in."

"I said I didn't want you in the house, but I knew you weren't going to give up. We're not in the house," she pointed out. "A small victory for my team."

"We aren't on different teams. Stop being difficult. Tobias wouldn't want the information if it wasn't important."

Sid didn't want to fight with Joe. The man deserved for her to leave him in peace. But what Tobias wanted was impossible to give, making clashing with her ex-partner—ex-lover—inevitable.

"Not everyone believes so implicitly in Strahan's theory." She kept her tone mild, reasonable.

Joe snorted. "You're talking about the Clan Primes who claim that he's crazy. They claim that the Clan boys are all that's needed to stand against evil. They just don't like Tobias letting the werefolk play superhero, too."

"There are Primes in the Dark Angels."

"Mostly from the vampire Families. And there are plenty of werefolk who don't like Tobias dragging their children into harm's way. I can't see *you* going along with all the arguments against the multiethnic makeup of the Dark Angels."

"Until the day comes when female vampires are asked to join, I'll have issues with your so-called open door policy. But I agree that the Primes you're talking about are arrogant jerks, and every species has jerks," she responded. "The Clans might be the most vocal in opposing your group, but it's true that there are Family vampires who don't like the Angels, either."

"The real objections, the fears, are because we make too much noise. We ask too many questions. We get results," Joe added. "We've stopped a lot of bad things from happening, and the Matri have quietly turned to us for hard solutions. Where do you think we get most of our funding?"

"I don't disagree that your group has done some good, or that the world is more dangerous than it's ever been—for mortal and supernatural people alike. I just don't think that mortals and immortals have formed any kind of conspiracy to bring down civilization."

"You haven't seen much of the evidence."

"I know that Strahan's been convinced of increasing interspecies evil ever since he walked away from that commercial airline bombing years ago. What *I* think happened is that he fell out of the sky and landed on his head."

"There's more than one conspiracy," Joe said, "whether you believe or not. People from every species are working together right now: some out of simple greed, some for political and ideological reasons." He gestured toward the burned-out mountains. "You saw the evidence."

Sid laughed softly. "Yes. You made sure we saw it."

Joe cleared his throat. "You noticed that, did you?"

"Scheming is something I'm very good at, so of course I noticed. I'm sure Eden did, too. But since we both believe Tobias's drug-dealing vampire conspiracy scenario, we're happy to help the Angels with that one."

Confusion warred with annoyance on Joe's features. "If you agree, why are you fighting us?"

She shook her head. "How many times do I have to say that I didn't pick up any information from the Manticores? I would have mentioned it back then if I did, when the Wolf Clan was following up on that incident."

"I see. You're being more loyal to your Clan than you are to the truth."

"How do you assume that from what I said?"

"Because I was there when the Manticores were brought down. I was part of the initial action."

"I know. I was there, too."

"Afterward I was told to mind my own business, and the Wolf Primes took responsibility for driving the rest of the Dawn dealers out of town. Laurent and Eden and I took down the Manticores—"

"Mom and I helped a little."

"And Cathy," he added. "It was our show. Then the great and mighty Wolf Clan stepped in. I remember that you disappeared for a couple of weeks following your rescue."

"That had nothing to do with the Primes hunting drug dealers. Mom and I were working on getting Laurent acknowledged as a member of the Clan. My only interest in the whole Dawn affair was to get my brother away from his lousy, stinking, disgusting Manticore sire's influence. You know this."

"What I know is that the Wolf Clan didn't go far enough in rooting out the evil. They stopped the drug trade in their own territory, but keeping Dawn out of San Diego didn't stop its manufacture. This arson shows that the Clan boys didn't finish the job."

"I'm not arguing with that. I'm sure Matri Juanita won't argue with it, either. Maybe some of the Clan Primes have gotten a little out of touch with the modern world."

"Those who haven't are joining the Angels."

Sid was finding the whole discussion circular and increasingly annoying. "Could we talk about something else? Or go back to not talking at all?" She stood up. "Even better, I'm going to bed. And in the morning you're going to be gone," she added.

Once again, she slipped inside faster than Joe could follow and locked the patio door firmly behind her. And shut the curtains to block the angry look on his face as he glared through the window at her.

She might have been going to bed, but she was sure she wasn't going to get any sleep.

Chapter Sixteen

December 16

*O*f course he'd broken in, and he knew that Sid knew it, but her bedroom door remained closed. After he swept up the glass from the small hole he'd made in the sliding door, Joe went into the living room.

He stopped in the doorway, perturbed. All of her living room furniture was different, and all the pieces were arranged differently. It was like he'd walked into a stranger's house, and it sent a chill through him.

What had she done that for? Not that changes in her life were any of his business.

He walked across the room and settled down on the new couch. Some of the lingering scents on the upholstery were familiar. He recognized members of his own family, Eden, Laurent, Lady Antonia, Tony Crowe. Other people had been here that he didn't know. One was obviously Sid's baby. There was the scent of a vampire Prime as well.

The male's identity was none of his business, Joe reminded himself.

He lay down and turned on his side. He'd already decided that the new furniture couldn't be as comfortable as the couch he remembered, but he was tired and was asleep in seconds.

He woke up to full daylight and no Sid stirring. A glance at his watch showed him that it wasn't that early. The couch had proved far more comfortable than his bedroll and he'd slept in. He stood up and roamed the room like a caged wolf while he waited for Sidonie.

He was fully aware that he was intruding on her privacy as he inspected everything within sight, smell, and sound, but maybe he'd find some important information that she wasn't consciously aware of. It was a pretty lame excuse, and he knew it. Never mind his righteous fury at her—being in her house made him seek familiar things to ease his homesickness.

Once, anywhere Sid was was home. It was almost a pity that the pain of her betrayal overwhelmed the pain of missing her.

Eventually Joe found himself standing before the shelf of framed photos. Her family; his family. Most of the pictures were new to him. Time had so obviously moved on for Sid, and the knowledge ground against his pain.

He wasn't represented anywhere in the picture collection. But there was one of the new male in her life.

"So you're Chuck," he said, picking up the picture.

Charles was a cute baby, but he didn't look much like a Wolf Clan cub. His hair was dark and curly, not wavy gold like Sid's or straight silver like Laurent's and Lady Antonia's. His eyes were dark, too. But he had Sid's smile and little baby Sid dimples.

Joe discovered he was smiling fondly at this stranger's son and put the photo down with a sudden frown.

When Sid's bedroom door opened, he turned to face her. The tousled hair framing her face and the outline of her body beneath a clinging red silk robe sent desire throbbing through him.

"I had hoped you wouldn't be here," she said.

"Who's the sire?" he sneered.

It was none of his business; he had no right to ask. But the jealousy that ate at him demanded to know.

Sid stared at him in open-mouthed shock. The hurt in her eyes bruised him and brought him back to his senses. If she'd chosen to rip his throat out he wouldn't blame her.

"I'm sorry," he said. "That was way out of line."

She closed her eyes for a moment, her expression an anguished mask. Joe couldn't help but take a step toward her, pulled by the urge to comfort as well as possess.

When she opened her eyes, they blazed with fury. When she spoke, her voice was low, but the tone was deadly. "I've stayed out of your life. Get out of mine."

Joe backed away with his hands held up before him. "I—"

Sid's bedroom door slammed, leaving the empty room echoing with all that wasn't spoken.

Joe was beginning to doubt Tobias's wisdom in giving him this assignment.

Sid sensed the moment Joe left the house, but her awareness of him was just as acute as if he was still there. How could it not be?

The mirror above her dresser revealed eyes full of bitterness and accusation. Damn, she hated feeling sorry for herself.

"It was an accident!" she reminded herself.

It was mindless lust, her conscience responded.

"It was love!"

That, too. It was still stupid. Dangerous.

But, oh, how lovely those few moments of abandon had been.

A rush of heated pleasure went through Sid as she watched Joe stretch. He stood naked in a shaft of sunlight with his back to her. She watched the play of the muscles of his arms and back, buttocks and thighs, and the sight took her breath away. Need grew in her, making her breasts heavy and her insides turn to flame.

But watching Joe brought out more than lust. Being with him brought her pure joy. He was so warm and real and alive! The sight of him heated her blood; his virile scent made her dizzy.

He glanced over his shoulder at her, and his bright eyes and come-hither look sent laughter bubbling through her.

"Why are you giggling, woman?"

"Because you're like champagne."

"Hmmph." Joe turned to face her and held out his arms. "Wouldn't you rather have good, red meat?"

Spoken from a werewolf to a vampire, this was terribly romantic. She came into his arms.

The hunger took her as skin touched skin. She

wanted—needed—so much more than his body. The hot blood pulsing through his veins called to her. The hunger as old as her species demanded what only Joe could give her.

Her fangs slid between her lips. The sensitive tips touched yielding flesh. She—

"Bit him," she said, trying to wipe the sensual haze away from the memory of the selfish, blasphemous act. Even though it had been the most orgasmic moment of her life.

Vampire females did *not* go around biting just anybody. Tasting anyone but a Prime was unthinkable. It was a breach of all that stood between survival and extinction of the species.

Sex with Joe had been one thing. But what she had done—

Sid shook her head. "I have done evil." Her reflection grinned back at her. "Okay, it didn't feel like it at the time. But I was very, very bad."

And she lived with the consequence, even if she'd never regret the action.

Chapter Seventeen

December 17, 8:00 AM

A battered old truck pulled into her driveway, deliberately blocking the carport, as Sid came out of the house. Joe had been gone for twenty-four hours, but here he was, back like a bad penny the moment she decided to leave the shelter of her home.

"Oh, come on!" she complained when she saw him sitting behind the wheel. Never mind that her heart flip-flopped at the sight of him, or that her body tingled with instant desire. "This has got to stop."

Joe got out of the truck and came up to her, presenting her with a tall paper cup of coffee. It smelled fresh and wonderful. "I was out of line yesterday," he said to her. "And I'm sorry."

She took a sip from his peace offering. "Where's the donuts?" she asked.

"In the truck." He tilted his head sideways. "Come on, I'll give you a ride to work."

Sid eyed his vehicle. "I don't know. I'm not sure I want to be seen in that thing in the daylight."

He canted an eyebrow at her. "Donuts," he coaxed. "And a cinnamon scone."

She laughed. "You know me too well."

His friendly expression didn't change a bit when he said, "I suspect I don't know you at all, but let's not go there right now."

Not knowing what to make of that, she got into the passenger seat without any more comment. She ate a donut and her scone and drank coffee while Joe drove. At least being a vampire meant she could indulge her sweet tooth without worrying about her figure.

She wasn't surprised when his route didn't take them anywhere near the Bleythin office. "I know very well that you aren't lost."

"We're just taking a short detour."

"I see."

He was wasting his time, but she decided not to waste her breath since he obviously wouldn't listen to anything she said. She watched the play of light and shadows through the palm trees lining the residential streets, pretending this was the old days—that they really were on their way to work or following a lead on a missing person. She knew it was stupid; she already missed those days too much. But it was better than thinking about where they were going.

Her imagination deserted her as she began to recognize the neighborhood, and she was tense when he pulled to a stop, knowing what she would see. She stared straight ahead.

There was a considerable silence before Joe said, "Where'd the house go?"

The house sitting on the lot was completely different than the one where she'd been held captive by the Manticore Tribe. The landscaping was also completely different.

A feral smile stretched her lips. "The old house burned down a couple of years ago."

It had been destroyed in a carefully controlled burn set by a professional arsonist. Her brother had some very interesting friends. The building was Laurent's, after all, to do with as he saw fit. Who was she to argue with how he chose to get rid of the bad memories the building represented? She'd brought the marshmallows.

"You might have mentioned this," he complained.

"You didn't tell me where we were going."

"You knew very well—"

She stuck the remaining donut in his mouth. "Shut up and eat. Of *course* no one mentioned it to you, in an e-mail or a voicemail or a text message or put some info on Facebook or wrote an old-fashioned letter which you'd never answer anyway," she added. "No one would talk to you about something when it might make you think of me. Everyone's been minding your bruised feelings for the last three years. You should thank them." She wagged a finger at him. "And send your family Christmas cards this year. They miss you. *I'm* the one who hurt you, stop taking it out on everybody else."

Joe stared ahead with his jaw clenched and his arms crossed over his chest. "You're right," he finally said. "I know it."

She hadn't expected this. "Really?"

"Hey, I may be *only* a werewolf, but I'm not completely stupid."

"What do you mean *only* a werewolf?"

It was hard work for Joe to hide a smile at Sid's indignant reply. She didn't hate him. She didn't disparage him. But his rejoicing still hit a painfully hard wall. Why the hell had she dumped him?

Not the time to go there.

He'd gotten enough information from her for now. Not from anything she'd said or done, but from the hormonal changes his delicate nose picked up scents that clearly spelled out her emotional turmoil.

Sidonie didn't like it here, and she most definitely didn't intend to talk about anything that had happened during her captivity. Ugly, dark emotions swirled around her; bad thoughts plagued her.

Why hadn't he noticed her agitation over the incident before? Years before?

Come to think of it, she'd never given more than the sketchiest of details of her time trapped among the Manticores. Sid was strong and smart and self-sufficient. It had never occurred to Joe that she'd suffered any trauma at the time.

Or maybe she'd wiped that from his memory, too. But he was aware of trouble now, and it was his duty to sniff it out.

"You can't lie to a nose," he warned her.

"What?" she asked.

Maybe it was more than duty. Maybe she needed help. Maybe he *wanted* to help her.

Damn it! He shouldn't be thinking like that.

"Nothing," Joe snapped. He put the truck in gear. "I'll take you to the office now."

Chapter Eighteen

"What do you call this color, dirty pink?" Joe asked as he stood in the center of the office and looked at the walls.

"Terra-cotta." Sid knew he wasn't going to like the changes to the agency office space, so why did it bother her?

He made a disgusted face. "Why are people always painting things?"

"To cover the bloodstains." She grinned when he gave her a sharp look. "Nah. I'm joking about that—this time."

The big room was full of desks, but they were the only people there.

"Where is everybody?" Joe asked.

"You know where Laurent and Eden are. Harry's on a case in Arizona. Cathy and Mike are off doing things with her werewolf/Romany relations. You remember them, yes?"

Joe nodded. "The Hunyara. Tobias is looking into recruiting among the ones Cathy is training."

"Do you know that our scientists are doing tests to figure out the basis of the Hunyara family's genetics? Maybe they can use the information to find more *cures* for the problems that plague us immortal types. Isn't science wonderful?"

Joe ignored her question as he walked up to the desk next to her own. "Who's using my desk?"

Sid bit her tongue on the answer that it hadn't been his desk for three years. "Dan."

He turned to her in surprise. "You're actually letting that flake work here? Officially?"

Sid put her hands on her hips. "That flake is my cousin."

Dan was the child of a Prime father and mortal mother, and was blessed, or more likely cursed, with the psychic ability to see the past.

"I don't have anything against Dan Corbett," Joe said. "He's my friend, but he's still a little . . . odd."

"Said the werewolf to the vampire. He's in much better control of his visions these days, and we've learned that his ability comes in handy when looking for lost things rather than lost people. At the moment, he's obsessed with the hunt for a scarlet egg."

Joe looked skeptical. "Dan's on an Easter egg hunt?"

She laughed. "Yes, actually. This egg was made as an Easter present. It's a gold and ruby Fabergé egg, presented to the last Russian czar in the early twentieth century. It went missing from an exhibit being set up by a private museum, and the curator approached us to quietly track it down before the exhibit opens."

"Dan's a historian. That's the sort of thing he would be good at finding."

Sid nodded. "He took off on his Easter egg hunt a week ago."

And a good thing, too, since her mortal cousin had been in a snapping, foul mood before the case came up. It was a relief to have him gone, especially with Joe now here to bug her. Of course, maybe she could have gotten Joe and Dan to go at each other while she snuck out the back.

Sid sat at her desk, ignoring Joe, while she read through several days' worth of e-mail.

She glanced his way when he pulled a chair up beside her. "Are you still here?" He plucked a framed photo of Charles off her desk.

"Hey!" she complained.

"He really is a fine-looking kid." Joe put the picture down. "I'm sorry I was rude about his sire. A werewolf has no business being jealous about who a vampire sleeps with."

His words were true, and they twisted like a knife in her gut. She kept her cool, suspicious that he was deliberately trying to upset her to get the information he really wanted.

"I have no idea who Charles's sire is." Which was true. "The Matri held an orgy. Everyone was invited." Which was not.

"Interesting lie," he observed.

"Damn it!" She sat back in her chair and glared at him. "Now I remember what you meant about the nose doesn't lie."

"You work with werewolves all the time."

"Yeah—but I forgot about *you.*" *I try not to think about you. I—* "Damn."

He folded his hands across his fine, flat stomach. "We could argue about us, but that won't get us anywhere." He leaned forward until their noses were almost touching and gazed into her eyes. "Tell me what the Manticores did to you."

Sid bumped her forehead against his as she sprang to her feet. "That is none of your—"

Her cellular phone began to play its "Tempting Fate" ringtone, and she gratefully flipped it open. "Hi, Dad. What's up?"

"She's gone!" Tony Crowe's frantic voice answered. "Rose is gone."

Sid's agitation was immediately replaced with sympathy for his loss. "I'm so sorry. But she was eighty—"

"No! I mean she's *gone*. Completely disappeared."

Okay—that didn't make any sense. "Explain to me exactly what you mean. What happened?"

Chapter Nineteen

December 16, 8:00 PM
Los Angeles, CA

"More roses have arrived for you, madam."

The enthusiasm in Gregor's Russian-accented voice made Rose Cameron smile. She didn't find smiling easy these days, not with the pain getting worse.

She put down her hairbrush and looked at Gregor's reflection in the mirror as he set the vase of red roses beside one full of white blooms. He had the grace of a cat, even with several dozen flowers in his arms. Gregor was movie-star handsome, and she knew movie stars. He was a fine, conscientious nurse—but this being Hollywood, he also had acting ambitions.

She thought that he'd have a great screen

presence with his strong features, black hair, and expressive green eyes, if this were the silent film era. When he'd first come to work at the nursing home a year ago, she'd worked with him to try to help him tone down his Russian accent before he went out on auditions.

"I heard the stories about your Christmas roses," he said.

The handsome young man turned slowly around to take in all the bright, fragrant blooms on every surface: red, white, yellow, pink, peach, even some faint green and pale lavender. The air was full of the heady scent; it almost masked the medicinal smells of the room she hadn't been able to leave for years.

"I didn't believe what I heard about Rose Cameron's Christmas," he went on. "I thought, *An anonymous admirer sends my favorite resident flowers every year, how sweet.* But I never expected he really sent enough to fill the whole room. You deserve them," he added as he faced her again.

She enjoyed his old-world style of flattery and didn't try to deny his assertion. She'd take all the compliments she could in the time she had left.

"Thank you, dear."

"And you really don't know who sends the roses? I wonder why your secret admirer isn't a

Hollywood legend, like the woman in black who leaves flowers at Valentino's grave."

Rose moved slowly toward her chair, and Gregor rushed to help her before she'd taken more than a step. She waited until she was settled in the comfortable wingback seat by the window before she answered.

"Legends grow up when people don't keep their private life private. Of course Valentino can't be blamed if a woman makes a spectacle of herself at his grave. She *wants* to be seen. I've always liked a quiet life."

"But wouldn't your secret admirer be thought of as a stalker in this day and age?"

"Maybe, but I've never had to worry about that sort of thing."

"Ah, of course. You were protected by the studio system."

Rose shook her head and cursed her failing body when the slight movement hurt. "There was someone on the L.A. police force who always looked after me."

Even surrounded by the gift of flowers, she didn't sigh romantically. Not only was she a fair actress, she'd had years of practice at keeping things to herself.

She turned a critical look on her handsome young nurse. "You didn't come here just to smell the roses, Gregor." She saw the needle he carried as he came closer. "No," she said. "No injection tonight."

"You know you need this," he said. "It will help you."

She knew there was no getting out of it, but that was no reason not to put up a fight. "I don't want the help. No one needs to live forever, Gregor. That's what you young people don't understand. You feel entitled to immortality—I know better."

"This is a very interesting philosophy, Madam Cameron, but it has nothing to do with your taking your medicine."

Talking made her tired. Everything was tiring. Still, pride and stubbornness made her give it one more try.

"I have the right to refuse a medical procedure if I wish."

"You should have that right," Gregor agreed. "But I'm afraid I can't let you. You need tonight's injection."

"Why? I don't want it."

"But I don't want you to die. Please take it for me, Madam Rose. You know how much I would miss you."

Rose was embarrassed at the way his charm worked on her. She always felt so much worse after the evening injection. She'd hoped to have this one night free of the blood-burning pain on top of the regular pain of having lived too long.

"My doctors are sadistic bastards."

"As doctors have been throughout the ages," he agreed. "May I give you the injection now?"

Oh, well, she'd put up with it for this long, she could take it a while longer.

"All right, Gregor." She presented her arm for the hated shot.

"Thank you, Rose."

He'd never called her by only her first name before and a wave of affection went through her. His touch was gentle as well as efficient as he administered the medication. She didn't feel the needle go in, but the fiery effect began instantly. Pain sliced through her, and everything around her went dark.

The scent of the flowers drew her back. When she opened her eyes Gregor was gone, and she breathed a sigh of relief at finally being alone. Rose smiled victoriously despite the pain. She was surrounded by flowers, it was December sixteenth, and she was determined to set her plan in motion. Now all she had to do was summon enough strength to get up and walk to the closet.

In 1956 she'd played Mary, Queen of Scots—in

a movie musical, of all things—with three broken ribs and pneumonia. It had not been her best performance, but she'd stubbornly gotten through the day-to-day hell of that shoot. Then there'd been the twisted ankle she'd limped on for miles in the Ardennes . . .

If you're going to commit suicide, get on with it before someone shows up to stop you, Rose chastised herself.

A great many kind people had worked hard not to let her go, so she was going to have to take care of it herself. As the pain had grown over the last year, she'd become more determined to find her way out.

Timing is everything, and you have to know when to make your exit. Now's the time.

She managed to rise to her feet and make her way across the room with slow, agonized steps.

It had taken her months of occasionally complaining of headaches to amass the supply of pills. She was certain that the medication she'd hidden in her fur coat's pockets was safe, since no one in Hollywood would dream of wearing chinchilla in this day and age.

She managed to get as far as turning the handle of the closet door when a man behind her said, "Going somewhere, sweetheart?"

At first, Rose told herself that she'd imagined it. Then she told herself that she didn't recognize his voice.

Finally, she turned slowly around and said, "Anthony Crowe, where have you been for the last sixty years?"

Chapter Twenty

Tony had been rehearsing for this moment for hours, for decades, for over half a century. But when he was finally standing face-to-face with Rose Cameron, all he could say was, "You look terrible."

Her famous indigo blue eyes were faded and they were surrounded by a sea of wrinkles, but they were still full of sharp intelligence and flashing with anger. This was not an auspicious start to their conversation.

"Of course I look terrible, you old fool." She looked him over critically. "Some of us do not have your . . . genetic advantages."

He held his hands out before him. "No—I

mean—when I was here last year, you still seemed pretty spry."

"I've been sick— What do you mean, *last year?*"

Her thin voice was raspy with pain, but the indignation came through loud and clear. Tony wanted to rush forward and take her in his arms, but she looked so fragile he feared the slightest touch would crush her.

He went to her and picked her up. She weighed nothing in his arms, but then, she never had. He carried her to the bed. Tall as she was for a woman of her era, she'd always been a skinny thing.

"You better not have anything romantic in mind," she told him.

He smiled. "You know I've never been much of a gentleman." He carefully set her on the bed and took a step back. "I have a lot of explaining to do."

Her anger didn't waver for a moment. "Start with telling me about last year. And the year before, and the year before that."

Tony perched beside her and took her hand in his. "Since you've been living here, I wait until you're asleep before I make my annual visit."

Rose breathed a quiet sigh. "So you have been watching me all these years. I didn't think I imagined it—that feeling of being protected, the occasional glimpse of movement out of the corner of my eye. You were there all along." She looked at him sternly. "But you weren't with me."

"I stayed away those years you were married. I didn't want to interfere with you having a normal life."

"Normal?" She laughed. "Thad Pearson was my best friend, but we never lived as man and wife. He was in a deeply committed relationship with another man. I was celibate. Neither condition was considered normal for movie stars and the press would have eaten us alive, so we covered for each other. We were happy sharing a house, but it wasn't a marriage."

"Oh." He winced with pain for her but couldn't help a certain amount of Primal pride when he asked, "You were really celibate?" She nodded. "That was stupid."

"I take it you weren't?"

He ducked his head, then looked up with a shameless grin. "Uh, no. It's not possible for my kind unless we're fully bonded. You *are* the love of my life," he added. "Were you really celibate?"

"I found the man I wanted when I was seventeen. Why settle for anyone less?"

"Stubborn female."

"Stop looking so pleased with your own prowess, Anthony Crowe. Don't think that it had all that much to do with you. I've never been a promiscuous person."

"Is that a hint of reproach I hear in your voice, old woman?"

"It's pain, older-but-still-gorgeous man." She touched his cheek. "I made my choice, but I never expected you not to take lovers." She stroked his cheek. "I'm glad you got rid of the goatee you grew after you retired. It didn't suit you at all."

"I guess I looked a bit too saturnine in—wait a moment. Retirement? Goatee?" He peered at her suspiciously. "What do you know about—"

"Private detective." She chuckled. "It wasn't as easy for me to keep track of your life as you did mine, but I managed. For the first few years, when you didn't keep your promise, I believed that you'd been killed in the war. Then I found the first newspaper article that mentioned your name."

"What newspaper—"

"Look in the top drawer, Anthony."

He left her side and returned carrying a shoe box. Rose watched him while he looked inside and found a small stack of newspaper clippings. In each article there was a mention of Officer Crowe, Detective Crowe, Detective III Crowe, or Detective Chief Crowe—his entire Los Angeles police career was boiled down to a few sentences in yellowed newsprint. There were a dozen photos as well, the earliest a faded Polaroid, the latest a digital print. Several of the older photographs showed him aging; the latest ones showed him as he actually looked, without the gray hair dye and makeup he'd worn during his last decade on the force.

He looked up in shock. "You've been keeping tabs on me!"

She laughed at his indignation. "Fair's fair, Anthony."

"How did you—"

"You told me you were moving to Los Angeles when we met, remember? And how if things worked out with the medicine, you'd like to join the police force after the war. My private investigator was very discreet. He said it wasn't hard to track your kind. He said he meant the romantic sort who sent anonymous bouquets from the same florist every year. But the way he said it made me suspect that he was a werewolf. Remember the ones we met in the forest?"

"I do. But—"

"You don't have to be concerned about your people's safety from me. There was never any discussion of anything supernatural between the detective and myself. What I know I will take to my grave. Take the box with you when you leave."

He put the box on the floor and took her hands

in his. "I'm not going anywhere." He kissed the palm of each hand. "I never wanted to leave you."

"You don't owe me any explanations."

"Which means you think that I certainly do, but you're being too polite to ask."

She tried to tug her hands from his, but he wouldn't let her go. "If I don't try to be polite, I'm going to start yelling and throwing things. Which will cause me to stroke out, which would send you into decades of despair and guilt—that might be fun for you, but I loathe melodrama."

He was acutely aware of the fury burning through her frail body, but he couldn't keep from teasing. "Come on, you know you'd love a great death scene."

"That's different. I intend to go gracefully, not croaking in the middle of a tantrum."

"You're not going anywhere, my darling. You are going to lie back and look lovely—"

He waited through her snort of derision.

"—and listen to what I have to say."

"It's past my bedtime."

"Stubborn wench."

They both smiled at the memories evoked by those words. Some of her tenseness relaxed and the expression in her eyes softened. She leaned against the pile of pillows at her back.

"All right, Anthony, I'll let you tell me a bed-time story."

The soul-deep happiness he felt being near Rose hadn't changed one iota. He'd known from the moment he'd found a frightened young woman hiding in a snow-covered thicket that she was the one he'd been meant to love. Their time had been stolen from them.

Not stolen—deliberately forbidden. *For the sake of the Clan.*

He sighed. "There is so much about my people that you don't know. Not that the opportunity to explain vampire culture presented itself while we were dodging Tiger tanks and German infantry. When I said good-bye to you in Paris, I didn't plan on it being for forever. I thought I'd find you after the war and tell you everything then."

"How romantic," she murmured. "Oh, don't look hurt, Anthony. I believe you, but—what on earth happened?"

"The simplest answer is that my Matri wouldn't let me have you. A Matri," he went on, "is the vampire female who rules each vampire Clan with total authority. We're a matriarchal society. I am Prime of the Corvis Clan. The Matri's word is law; her decisions are literally life and death ones."

"You got caught in some sort of political in-fighting, didn't you?"

"How perceptive of you, my darling."

"Making movies is a political process. Anything with a power structure involves politics, especially in uncertain times. After the war we had to deal with the death of the studio system, McCarthy, television. What did vampires have to deal with?"

"When I came home from the war there was a lot going on within the Clans; modern ideas were starting to undermine ancient traditions. I'd helped start some of that undermining and wasn't exactly in favor at home."

"The medicine you were taking to try to stay outside in the daylight got you in trouble?" she asked.

He nodded. "Good guess. If you'll recall, it didn't work all that well once the fog and clouds cleared up. But it did help some, and it was the beginning of a new way of life for our people. We'd spent thousands of years living in the dark, and not everybody was in favor of living any other way. My Clan Matri was—"

Tony bit his tongue on the many unpleasant things he thought about the last Corvis Matri. She'd had good reasons for every hurtful decision, from her generation's point of view. He still hated her, but he'd had sixty years to come to understand her.

He settled on saying, "Conservative. She probably felt the world was turning upside down—her daughter was living with a mortal male, the Primes were clamoring for her to invest in medical research, and I'd run off to fight with the American army when Primes weren't supposed to do that sort of thing."

"You told me that vampires had always defended mortals."

"Yes, but until the use of daylight drugs, we'd fulfilled our vows by helping people on a one-to-one basis. Once the drugs that let us dwell in daylight became practical, the Primes began to join the military, and they began taking sides in mortal affairs."

"They became American citizens? They served country instead of Clan?"

"Something like that. Some of the Matris were certainly scared of losing our loyalty—and of conflicts with Primes in other countries who were loyal to their own causes. It didn't work out like that; diplomacy prevailed. But there was tension at the time."

"And you started it?"

"Let's say that my Matri didn't think I'd set a good example when I defied ancient tradition by playing a grunt in khaki instead of an elite knight in shining armor."

Rose smiled. "That's true. The tank we stole wasn't very shiny."

"So when I announced that the mortal I'd found to be my bondmate was a movie star, my Matri used your fame as a reason not to allow me to complete the bond."

"What?" Rose sat up straight, although the movement obviously brought her pain. "She forbade us from being together because she decided the publicity associated with my life would 'out' all vampires?"

"That is the exact reasoning she used."

"And you went along with this?"

It broke his heart to answer. "I had no choice."

"Oh, really?"

Rose reached for the bowl of roses on the bedside table and hurled them at his head.

Chapter Twenty-one

Anthony caught the vase in a blur of speed that made Rose dizzy. He set the roses back on the table without even a drop of water spilled.

"Show-off," she complained.

He pressed a finger to her lips. "Someone might hear a crash. We don't want to make a ruckus, do we, darling?"

"Shhh . . ." He waited a moment before taking his hand away from her mouth. "If you make a ruckus, we might be heard."

Rose turned to look at her protector. Face-to-face, close together, she reveled in the warmth of his body and the virile masculine scent beneath the dirt that covered them both. There was also the unmistakable scent of blood.

"If I was screaming, it was because you were shot," she said.

"No, I wasn't."

Oh yes, he had been. She'd seen how he'd jerked as the bullets stitched a line across his body. When he'd gone down, she'd believed he'd never get up again. The loss had sliced through her. She hadn't known she was screaming until his hand covered her mouth. His rough touch sent joy leaping through her.

There was a certain feral gleam in his eyes as he studied her face. He looked hungry. It was hard to breathe with him looking at her like that. It was freezing in the ruined farmhouse, but the temperature around them rose significantly.

"I thought they'd killed you," she went on.

"I was just dodging bullets."

"You were bleeding." She touched one of the spots where gunfire had left holes in his dark jacket. Her fingers came away smeared in red. "See?"

He put his hands on her shoulders. "It's nothing. Don't worry about it."

He glanced toward the dead German blocking the doorway, then led her out of the ruined kitchen, into a roofless area that had once been a bedroom. Snow fluttered down from the night sky overhead and swirled around this abandoned place.

Anthony went absolutely still, listening. "There's no once else out there. We're safe for now."

She felt safe being with him, but maybe she was kidding herself. "You are what I think you are, aren't you?"

He turned his gaze on her, and his eyes glittered in the night. His voice was a dangerous whisper. "What do you think I am?"

Rose wouldn't turn away, no matter how dominating his stare. Tension stretched between them. She could no longer feel the cold. The snowflakes that occasionally touched her skin might as well have been burning ash.

"I don't want to say what I think—what I know—you are."

He stepped so close to her that their steamy breath mingled. "What am I, Rose?"

"Hungry."

The word itself granted him permission. His mouth touched hers in one swift kiss and then moved down to her throat. Her scarf and coat and shirt were all pushed aside. Cold touched her exposed skin for a moment. Only a small spot of skin was uncovered, but she'd never been more *naked. Longing blended with intense pleasure when his lips touched her throat.*

She needed more. Her hand came around the back of his head, pressing him closer. "Anthony . . ."

There was a second of sharp pain, then—

Her bones melted. They turned to molten gold.

Her blood burned. Pleasure sang in every vein and artery.

Her flesh was on fire. Rapture danced through the flames.

The world shattered; she became whole.

He was there with her and they were whole together. One.

His need consumed her. Her giving gave her everything.

Just before the ecstasy became unbearable she thought, So this is what an orgasm is like.

Sweetheart, you haven't felt anything yet, *Anthony's thought answered her.*

"Oh, my," she said. She was breathing heavily.

Rose tried to open her eyes and realized that they weren't closed. The darkness filling her vision came from the depths of Anthony's eyes. She blinked and the rest of his beloved face came into focus.

Rose fanned her face with her hand. She was warm in several unexpected ways. "Anthony, I'm not sure it's appropriate for a woman my age to feel like this."

"I'm older than you," he reminded her. "And I like how I feel just fine." He grinned. "And accomplished without the need for Viagra."

"That was . . . nice," she said. "Possibly a bit icky, if I think about it too closely, but nice."

"It's our memory to share."

She brushed her hand across his cheek, too aware of its wrinkled crone shape against the smoothness of his skin. "A lovely memory. Thank you for it—but don't think it excuses you in any way."

"Excuses me from what?"

"From abandoning me, you damned fool. Look at you. Look at me. Don't you dare tell me that you're here now, because your sudden appearance does nothing to make up for the years in between."

"Darling, if I had claimed you against my Matri's command, there wouldn't have been any years in between. Those who break the rules pay with their lives—my people are vampires, you know."

"We could have arranged an accident, made it look like we were killed."

"I considered it, believe me, but the chances

of our being discovered were too high. I wasn't going to put your life at risk. My death sentence would have been your death sentence as well. I didn't drag you out of the Battle of the Bulge just to get you killed because I was too selfish to live without you." He stroked her hair and bent to kiss her cheek. "But I'm too selfish to live without you anymore."

Rose was too aware that her hair was silver and thin, that her cheek was a wrinkled ruin. She didn't know if Anthony saw her as she was or as he remembered her, but she was under no illusions. It made her heart sing that to him she would always be beautiful, but it didn't make her weak heart any healthier. Nor did it stop the pain that shot through her with such sudden violence that she couldn't stop the moan she didn't want him to hear.

"What's the matter?"

Her vision had gone out of focus but she knew that Anthony's face was close to hers. "What do you think's the matter? I'm dying, you idiot."

"Not on my watch, you aren't."

She managed a laugh despite the agony.

A moment later he said, "Here."

Something hard was thrust against her lips. Then a hotsweetmetallic flavor was on her tongue. Familiar. Longed for.

It was too late for this! It was a waste!

But once she tasted Anthony's blood, she could no more stop herself than she could stop the pain. Or the love that had been part of her for so very long.

Rose's need was unbearable, and all she could do was drink.

Chapter Twenty-two

December 17, 1944, 12:40 AM
Ardennes Forest, Belgium

This was not a pleasant evening for a stroll in the forest. Though Tony wasn't likely to get frostbite, his body's resistance to cold didn't stop him from hating it. The wind whipped snow against his face with burning force; his eyelids felt frozen open. It was just not a nice time to be outdoors.

It wasn't only the foul weather Tony found irritating; there were also all those enemy soldiers sharing the woods with him. Sometimes they shot at him, but it was the overwhelming noise of gun and mortar and cannon fire that really annoyed him.

As he moved cautiously through the invasion, observing and memorizing all he saw, counting *heartbeats and drinking in the scent of blood, he couldn't help but recall the almost casual order that had brought him on this scouting expedition.*

"Go up to the Belgian Front and have a look around for me, Crowe. See if there's anything to the rumors of a German buildup on the other side of the Ardennes Forest," the general had said, puffing on a cigar. "It won't take long; there's nothing really going on, just some exaggerated reports from the green troops training up there who think they hear ghosts in the woods. You'll be back in Paris long before Christmas."

The general's nothing had turned out to be a hell of a lot of something.

As Tony was about to turn around and head back to the jeep he'd left in a village many miles to the rear, a girl's voice stopped him between the shelter of one tree and the next.

Hide over here. It's safer.

As bullets whizzed past his head, Tony dove to the ground and peered over the dubious shelter of a tree stump to look around.

Where's here? *he thought back.*

Straight ahead. Close your eyes and you'll see me.

He understood exactly what she meant and did as she said. When he blocked out all the hubbub around them he immediately sensed her

*heartbeat, the warmth of her flesh, the aroma of
her blood. And what a lovely aroma it was!*

Even more delicious was the aura of a frightened, strong, stubborn, and very sharp mind.

She was also very young.

He opened his eyes and crawled to a clump of
bushes only a few feet away.

When he reached the mortal girl curled up in
the middle of the thicket, he asked, How long
have you known you were a telepath?

A what?

Ah. So she didn't know what she was doing.
Crisis sometimes brought out latent talents.

When she looked at him, he saw that she was
surprised to see him. He saw fear in her huge
eyes, but not fear of him. Her instant trust caught
at his heart.

"Who are you?" he whispered. "What are you
doing here?"

"Rose Cameron. I'm with the USO."

Of course she was. There were several troupes
of entertainers up here, in what was supposed
to be a safe area, giving shows to help the boys
celebrate Christmas.

He looked her over carefully, seeing her clearly
in the darkness. "What are you doing in the USO?
Do you have a note from your mother to be in
this war? How old are you? Fifteen?"

"I'm twenty!" Her voice never rose above a faint whisper, but she put a shout's worth of indignation into it. He cocked an eyebrow and stared her down. "Seventeen," she admitted, but she was still indignant.

He took her hand. "We're between waves of soldiers for the moment. Let's get out of here."

She shook her head. "I can't."

"Don't worry, I'll—"

"My ankle," she interrupted. "I don't know if it's broken or just twisted, but I can't walk any farther. You go. I'll be okay."

They were surrounded by an invading army. It was a bitter cold night during the worst winter of the century. She was not going to be okay, and they both knew it.

When she tried to tug her hand from his, he didn't let her go.

He pulled her from hiding and picked her up. "Don't worry, Rose. You won't slow me down."

"Hey," she complained as he held her close. "I don't snuggle up to total strangers."

"My name's Anthony Crowe," he told her. "And I'm going to take care of you."

His heart told him that he'd been waiting to take care of her all his life.

Chapter Twenty-three

"Feeling better?" Anthony asked. His voice sounded as though it came from a great distance, perhaps at the other end of a long, lighted tunnel.

"Yes," Rose said.

In a way, she was feeling better, emotionally. Physically—the pain hadn't gone away, but it was different, bearable. She felt more alive.

She found that she was no longer propped up by pillows but tucked in the crook of Anthony's arm. Her head rested on his chest. Like a young girl snuggled up with her lover.

"This feels good," she admitted. "I haven't been warm in a long time." After a while, she said,

"I'd forgotten about using telepathy when we met. Are you sure I really shared thoughts with you?"

"I'm sure."

"It's never happened with anyone else."

"I should hope not—it was meant for me."

"Arrogant man."

"I am. Besides, you channeled your psychic talent into your acting."

It took Rose some restraint not to point out that she might have preferred to channel her talent into making babies and a home with him. There was no use crying over spilled milk; she was content with what she had right now. But she was also exhausted.

"I think you should leave now, Anthony," she said.

"I'm comfortable." His voice sounded drowsy. He yawned. "I think I'll stay right here."

"Nonsense. You'd shock the nurse when she brings my three AM meds."

"What? Do they wake you up to give you sleeping pills?"

"Something like that. You really should go now." She didn't want him to go, but she didn't want him to stay.

"Have it your way, my love." He rose to his feet, as lithe and lively as a young man should be. "Where shall we go?"

She slapped at him when he reached down to pick her up. "We aren't going anywhere. Just go."

It finally began to dawn on him that she meant it. He looked like a hurt little boy, which made her want to hug him and tell him that everything was all right. But putting her arms around him would break her, physically and mentally. She'd never let him go, or she'd never stop crying if she did. Neither was acceptable at this point.

Anthony crossed his arms and cocked his head to one side. "You're playing hard to get. That's not your style."

She decided to go along with this game. "I never was easy, Anthony. If you think you can donate a little blood and then just move in, you're mistaken. It'll take more than a pint to win me over after all this time."

"What about all the roses?"

"They're a lovely romantic gesture. But still not enough."

"Is it a courtship you want?"

"I think I deserve one."

"Shall I bring chocolate next time? Champagne?"

"I'm not averse to diamonds."

He kissed her hand. "The hard stuff it is, then."

He gave her a puppy dog look designed to make her relent. She smiled and shook her head.

"Good night, then, my winter Rose."

She managed not to snicker at this blatant ploy. "Good night, Anthony."

She only hoped she still had the strength to make it to the closet and the hidden pills once he was gone.

Chapter Twenty-four

December 17, 11:00 AM

From the outside, Ocean View Retirement Center was a very pleasant place. It was a large hacienda-style building set in beautifully landscaped gardens and surrounded by a low wall. There really was an ocean view, although a freeway cut across the grounds and the cliff overlooking the water. The place offered lovely rooms, a large professional staff, and excellent care for the elderly. Ocean View was a perfectly pleasant environment in which to wait for death.

Tony knew that Rose received the best possible care there, yet he hated this prison for her aging body with his heart and soul.

I should have taken her out of there last night,

he thought. *I should never have fallen for her "I want a courtship" ploy.*

He shook his head, irritated with himself and a little bit with Rose, and a wave of love for her washed over him. *She hasn't changed a bit,* he thought fondly. He knew she'd been more worried for him than she was for herself. She'd always been that way; quick to notice his problems and quick to try to fix them.

"We're going to have to stop soon," the girl in his arms said.

He smiled despite the pain, amused because he was carrying a Rose. "I'm fine," he told her.

"You're not," she answered. *"You're flinching more with every step."*

"I'm fine. You don't weigh anything."

"It's not me. You've been in pain since the sun came up."

"What sun?" he asked. The snow had stopped, but clouds and fog obscured the shadows of the deep woods even further.

"What little light there is hurts you. You need to get under cover."

He wore a helmet, gloves, and boots, a scarf covered most of his face, and his body was protected by a uniform and a heavy coat, but he was suffering from hell's own sunburn. He didn't know if what was happening to his eyes was called snow blindness or sun blindness, but pretty soon he wasn't going to be able to see a thing.

"You're hurting, Anthony."

How could she know? It must be another example of the telepathy she wasn't aware of.

He'd been using his extra senses to avoid the enemy, swerving in long zigs and zags to avoid any German patrol he heard. There'd been plenty of gunfire, but he managed to keep them away from numerous firefights in the woods and villages around them. The result was that they'd spent a dangerous amount of time out in daylight. But heading in a straight line would have been more dangerous to her. He'd cope with the damage, but at some point his growing thirst was going to send him into a frenzy.

"I'm going to get you to safety," he told her.

"Of course you are," she said. "But wouldn't it be best to hide out until nightfall?"

"It'll be too cold for you to travel at night."

She laughed. "I'm from a ranch in northern Montana. I could teach you a thing or two about surviving in the cold."

Sometimes he forgot that mortals weren't as fragile as they seemed. "All right. Let's find somewhere to hide."

It wasn't long before they came across an abandoned shed. Tony ducked through the doorway and set her down. Rose closed the rickety door behind them, completely blocking out the dim daylight. Tony sighed in relief and sank to his knees.

His vision cleared quickly and the first thing he saw was her worried expression and her steady, assessing gaze. Goddess, but she was beautiful! She was a skinny kid with frizzy copper hair and freckles, but she had great bone structure and huge dark eyes.

"They're actually blue. Your eyes look black, but they're dark blue. Amazing."

"You see in the dark. That's even more amazing."

He didn't try to explain away this ability. He reached into an inner coat pocket and brought out the bottle of precious pills. The daily dosage was supposed to be two; he popped down three. The burns were already healing in the darkness; he hoped the medicine would make the blood thirst more bearable. Frankly, he wasn't sure if the stuff did any good at all. His fangs ached every time he looked at the girl.

"We'll rest here for a while. I'll keep watch. Get some sleep, Rose."

She limped away from the door and settled

down beside him. He was pleasantly surprised when her arms came around him. "We'll share body heat for a while first," she said. "You're freezing."

"Naturally low body temperature." He put his arms around her waist and pulled her closer. "Your warmth feels wonderful."

"Will the pills help you? What's a sick man doing out here anyway?"

"Until yesterday, this was supposed to be the safest area in the war," he reminded her. "Weren't you here to entertain the wounded?"

"Yes, but what are you doing here?"

"Gathering intel," he said. "I was supposed to have a quick look around and get out."

"I'm sorry your quick look turned into a rescue mission."

He pulled her even closer. "I'm not. I'm going to get you out, Rose. We'll be fine."

I'm going to get you out now, too, Tony thought as the memory faded. He chuckled and patted the pocket holding the diamond ring as he walked toward the gate of the Ocean View Retirement Center. He'd never pulled off an escape from an old folks' home before.

Chapter Twenty-five

The smell of fresh paint wasn't unpleasant but it was unexpected, especially as it grew stronger with each step closer to Rose's room. Tony expected the scent of roses, but there was no hint of the abundance of bouquets in the air. A heavy dread came over him, the anxiety so strong it muffled all his other senses. The hallway was long and wide, lit by recessed lighting and tall windows at either end, painted pastel blue and hung with cheerful landscape prints. It was also utterly empty, and although he knew his footsteps were silent he could hear them echoing in his head.

"Rose?" he whispered as he reached her door.

The door was open and the smell of paint wafted from inside, almost nauseating him as it hit him in the face. The room was empty. No furniture. No bed. No rugs on the floor. No pictures on the clean white walls. No curtains on the windows. No roses.

No Rose.

Tony took a bewildered step inside.

Where was Rose?

Confusion swirled around him, causing genuine dizziness, not a sensation he was used to. The square of sunlight coming in the bare window had moved slightly by the time his head cleared enough to realize someone was speaking to him.

"Sir?" a woman asked. "Sir, are you all right?"

Tony turned to the doorway, where a young woman in one of those ridiculously cheerful print tunics was looking at him in concern.

Where's Rose Cameron? he demanded, sending the words straight into the mortal's mind.

"Who?"

She thought the word as well as spoke it, her confusion completely genuine.

Damn!

His anger caused her pain, and for a moment he didn't care. Then Tony took a step back, took a deep breath, and resumed the civilized façade he normally used when dealing with mortals. "I'm

Doctor Crowe," he told her as he looked into her eyes. "I'm looking for one of my patients, but I seem to have been directed to the wrong room. I need to look at your files."

"Of course." She smiled pleasantly and led him to a nurses' station located in the circular atrium where all the halls met.

Along the way, Tony sent out telepathic feelers to every mortal within reach. He asked them all, *Where's Rose?* The answers he received concerned bushes, plants, gardens, and floral arrangements. There was nothing to do with longtime resident Rose Cameron in any of their heads.

This is crazy!

The terror racing through him made it hard to think. It made it even harder to control his temper. His impulse was to tear the place apart with his bare claws until he found the woman he loved.

Instead he asked to look through the nursing home's files when he got to the central desk, and looked through the computer records and filing cabinets with the same results he'd found in the mortals' minds.

Nothing.

If she'd ever existed, there was no record of it here.

If she'd never existed, why had his heart been twisted with pain for all these years? If she'd never existed, why had no lover but her ever given him the completion his soul craved?

He became aware of the people gathered in the atrium watching him. Not with hostility or wariness or guilt; not a single negative emotion was directed at him. There was curiosity, brief relief from everyday work boredom, even some female appreciation for his looks. But nothing in their awareness had anything to do with Rose.

He looked back at them with total hostility. He wanted to rip into them and spill their blood. He wanted to shred their minds to tatters and flay them alive. He wanted answers. He wanted Rose.

He wanted to kill in reaction to the pain and the panic. It was a Prime's right to have what he wanted!

He reminded himself that he was not a child. What use were all the years spent in the Clan crèche learning to control his instincts if he broke now when Rose needed him most?

He rose slowly to his feet, made his clenched fists relax.

"Thank you," he said to the watching staff.

Tony walked out of the Ocean View Retirement Center, fear and rage rising with every step. By the time he reached the street, he was seeing everything around him in shades of blood. When he stepped from shade into sunlight, his skin flared with pain and the world went completely red.

It was the mundane ringing of the cellular telephone in his coat pocket that brought Tony back to the mortal world. He became aware that he was standing at the corner of a busy street, but he had no idea where he was. He must have walked here. He glanced up at the street sign and got his bearings. The phone kept ringing.

He had no interest in talking to anyone but answered it for the sake of silence. "What?"

"There's a situation at the clinic," Dr. Casmerek answered. "I need you here right now."

The mortal doctor was usually a very cool customer. He was used to caring for vampires suffering from everything from splinters to drug-induced psychoses, so he needed to be calm and authoritative. Casmerek didn't sound like either of those things at the moment.

"I'm busy," Tony told him brusquely, but duty made him add, "What's the problem?"

"Busy?" Casmerek shouted. "You are head of clinic security and you are needed here. Now!"

Tony hated the pull of responsibility nagging at him. He had his own problems, damn it!

"I asked what was wrong."

"Bomb threat to the clinic," Casmerek answered. "It was called in to the Los Angeles police; now I've got a swarm of *mortal* police combing through a *vampire* clinic."

A roar filled the speaker, and Tony pulled the phone away from his head.

"Oh, my God! It wasn't a threat!" Casmerek shouted. "Tony!"

Tony closed his eyes for a moment as helplessness and hopelessness washed through him. "On my way."

Why was he always forced to choose between Rose and his people? This was a real emergency and he couldn't abandon them. And he wasn't going to abandon her.

But there were no rules that said he couldn't ask for help.

He dialed Sidonie's work number. He had a missing person, and his daughter was a missing persons investigator.

Chapter Twenty-six

December 17, 2:00 PM
San Diego, CA

"*Y*ou can't just leave!" Joe insisted.

Sid pretended not to notice that he'd followed her into her room, though it was hard to ignore a werewolf pacing around her bed as she tried to pack.

Her first mistake had been to let him drive her home after Tony's call. Somehow he'd willfully and stubbornly gotten the false impression that she'd left the office for the day, not that she intended to leave the city. Even after she'd told him she was going to Los Angeles.

"You are *not* going to Los Angeles," he said. Again.

Sid stopped stuffing underwear into a suitcase

pocket and looked at him. "I am a missing persons detective. I have a client who happens to be my sire, who has reported a missing little old lady to me. To me. I'm going to help him find Rose Cameron."

"Rose Cameron? The movie star from the forties and fifties? How could she be missing? I didn't know she was still alive. I remember that you once made me sit through a marathon showing of all of her old films. You never mentioned she had any connection to your sire."

Sid remembered that evening very well, and very fondly, as she did all the times they'd been comfortable in each other's company. They'd curled up next to each other on the couch with all the lights out and gone through an entire boxed set of classic DVDs. It was how they'd unwound from a hard case that hadn't turned out well.

"What Tony told me in private stayed private, but I wanted to see what she was like when I rented those three films. At the time, you said watching her movies was fun. And those were only her most famous ones."

"I enjoyed the wine and the popcorn," he admitted. "She was certainly a beautiful woman in her time. The musical sucked."

"A lot of those 1950s Technicolor extravaganzas haven't aged well, but that's not the point.

The point is that to Tony, she's the woman who should have been his bondmate. And he wants her back safe and sound."

"Back from where?"

"I don't know that yet."

"But—I don't understand. If they aren't bonded, how could—"

"Sometimes you can't be with who you want to be with, all right? People don't always get to live happily ever after. Life can be complicated—even for a vampire!"

She knew from the look on his face that her vehemence had told him too much.

She picked up her travel case. "My father needs me."

He blocked the door. "Tobias needs your memories."

"Tobias can go to hell." She looked the werewolf up and down. He was tall and whipcord lean but with wide shoulders. He was strong and fast in his human form, and deadly fierce in wolf shape. "You know I could toss you aside like a rag doll," she told him.

He nodded. "But you're not the impulsive, violent type. You're sneaky, but you're not mean."

"I'll take that as a compliment, but you still better get out of my way."

Joe's stern expression relaxed. He actually

smiled as he held out his hand. "Why don't you let me carry the luggage?"

His smile twisted her heart, and the temptation to kiss those smiling lips nearly overwhelmed her. He had such a beautiful mouth. Damn him!

All she meant to do was hand him the bag. But their hands touched and their eyes met, and the air sizzled between them. The bag dropped on the floor.

Joe kicked it aside, then reached for her—and she couldn't turn away.

"Oh, hell," Sid said as she came into his arms.

His body was stiff with reluctance, pride fighting desire, but his mouth came down on hers, hard and demanding.

Sid's response was just as demanding, even more desperate. Too many years of missing him, needing him, made her reckless and greedy. He was the only one who could fill the emptiness in her soul, who could make her body come alive.

She was alive now, so alive it hurt. Being alive hurt. So what? It was wonderful! She welcomed that pain, along with every other denied sensation.

I've missed you, wanted your touch. It's been so long . . .

She'd dreamed about making love to Joe, fantasized about it, survived on memories. This very real kiss took her by storm.

He reacted just as wildly, picking her up and tossing her beneath him on the bed. For a moment she almost panicked when his weight came down on her, but she remembered that this was Joe. *Her* Joe. No silver manacles bound her. Her hands were free to roam over him, to help him pull his shirt off, to press her skin to his. She was free to kiss his face, the hollow of his throat, his chest.

She concentrated on everything she could see and touch, used her fascination with his body to ignore the heated roar of his blood and the drumming of his heart. She could have only so much of him, and no more. She would not be a vampire with him. Never again.

Her clothes came off as quickly as his. His wide-eyed shock at the sight of her flesh brought a smile to her lips.

"What the devil have you done to your arms?" Joe demanded.

He referred to the sharply angled sepia tattoos that wound like bracelets around her toned biceps.

"Sexy, aren't they?" she asked.

"Uh"—Joe stroked the marked skin with his thumbs—"yeah."

She chuckled throatily and turned onto her stomach. Joe gasped at the markings that emphasized the length of her back and the curves of her lower body.

"Sweet mother . . ." he murmured in a voice almost strangled with lust.

"Touch them," she urged.

He did just that, and she loved the way he breathed her in while he stroked and kissed the geometric swirls on her arms and back and hips. He explored the fresh tattoos, and the rest of her, with a thoroughness that was maddeningly pleasurable.

Sid arched against him, opened herself to him. She kept her lips firmly shut over aching fangs. Tasting him was one desire she would fight off. Heat rose between them, flowed through her, and she gave herself to the sensation.

Explosive pleasure took her when he entered her, but need began to curl toward a fresh orgasm instantly. It had been so long, and he was—

"Joe."

It was all she could say, though it meant so much more than a name.

"Bitch," he answered.

She loved hearing that word from his lips. From his kind it was not an insult; the harshly spoken word held all the possessiveness she longed for. She was his. At least for this moment, and it was all she wanted.

As he claimed her with hard, demanding strokes. She was surprised at how much she reveled in the roughness of their wild coupling, in the way they marked each other, scratch for scratch, bruise for bruise. She loved the way the orgasms mixed with the pain.

She'd longed for this—the way she shrieked and he roared when he exploded inside her, and how they were one, together, for that long, delirious moment.

Chapter Twenty-seven

*J*oe slowly came back to himself, up out of a dark well of total bliss. He sat up and swung his legs over the side of the bed, then wiped the sweat-dampened hair from his face while he stared bleakly at the floor. His body sang with life and satisfaction. His soul was shell-shocked.

"What the hell was I thinking?"

"What does that mean?"

"You're the last person in the world I want to make love to."

"Then pretend I'm somebody else," she answered.

He knew what she meant. She certainly looked

different, at least with her clothes off. "Maybe I will," he said.

Sid's emotions brought swift changes in body chemistry that came to him as the scent of hurt, quickly followed by anger. "Then just think of it as good rough sex with a stranger. Or think of it as part of your mission."

It was his turn to ask, "What does that mean?"

"That you were thinking of your duty while we did the deed," she answered. "It was the Dark Angels version of lying back and thinking of England. In the active, aggressive way of your unit."

The stinging sarcasm in Sid's voice made him turn to look at her. The sight of her naked body sent renewed desire through him. Anger at his own lack of control made him lash out at her, even while a part of him recognized that her sarcasm was trying to cover pain. "What are you talking about?"

"Everything we've been doing"—she glanced at the bedside clock—"for the last hour was to distract me, delay me. You set a trap to keep me from leaving, and I walked right into it."

Joe shot to his feet to glare down at her. That she was a beautiful naked female exuding the intoxicating aromas of sex served to make his anger hotter. Fury kept his mind off what his body wanted to start all over again.

How could she *dare* think he'd try to use her? How could she believe he'd use sex as a weapon?

"I don't play that kind of game, Sidonie. Not even for the sake of an assignment."

"Oh, yes," she sneered. She sat up and wrapped her arms around her knees as she looked over his naked form. "You always play fair."

"I'm not you."

She didn't flinch at this nasty jab. She got up on the opposite side of the bed, stretched, and rolled the stiffness from her shoulders.

He saw that he'd left her with bruises that were already healing. He felt the scratches she'd left on his back while she clutched and clawed through her orgasms.

"Where are you going?" he asked when she started from the bedroom.

She glanced back over her shoulder. "To Los Angeles. But I'm going to get cleaned up first."

He followed her into the bathroom and into the shower.

"What the hell are you doing?" she demanded.

"Saving time and hot water." Joe turned on the tap and tossed her the shampoo. He squirted shower gel into his cupped palm. To prove that he really hadn't been trying to distract her, he added, "We'll make up the time already lost on the drive."

"Fine," she grumbled. She spread lather onto his chest. "It's too late to argue now."

He looked at her glistening wet skin. It was none of his business, but he couldn't stop the questions. "Why the ink? When did you—"

"Don't worry, it won't last," she told him. "I needed a certain trashy, edgy look for an undercover job, so I opted for a lot of ink. Eden went with me for moral support when I had them done last month and ended up getting a tattoo on her hip."

"A volcano?" he guessed. "To surprise Laurent?"

She smiled and nodded. "Our lava-loving Eden went for a tasteful tattoo of Mount Fuji."

"How'd the op go?"

She gave a fierce grin. "Not only did we find the kidnapped teenager we were looking for, we brought down the cult that took her." She traced a finger around the design circling one arm. "It's mortal ink and will fade in a few months."

He was delighted the tats weren't permanent. Even though it was none of his business, he preferred Sid's naked body clean and unmarked and—

All he had meant to do was share some of the soap with her, but his hand slipped when he touched Sid's chest, and the next thing he knew his palm was covering her breast. She arched against him, her nipple going hard against his palm. He went stiff as well, his erection pressing against her thigh. Her hand came around his penis. Joe had a momentary rush of terror, but instead of causing him agony, Sid stroked a groan of pleasure from him.

"Goddess," he muttered. "Here we go again."

Sid's face was pressed against his shoulder, her voice muffled over the rush of water. "What is the matter with us?"

"I really do want to keep my hands off you," he told her. But he couldn't stop touching her, tracing the sensual lines of ink that marked her body, roaming over her breasts, her ass, between her wet thighs.

"My sire needs me," she protested weakly.

"We'll make it quick," he promised.

Sid lifted her head to look into his eyes. "You still hate me, right?"

"Completely."

"Good."

"You still think I'm trying to stall you?" he asked.

"Doing a good job of it, too."

"Nothing's changed." They said it together.

He wanted to believe that he could make love—at least have sex—with Sid and not feel anything but hatred for her. He knew he was lying. Maybe she was, too. It didn't matter. He had to have her or die.

She hooked a leg around his hip, and guided him into her. "Don't worry," she whispered in his ear. "I'd never let you die."

Chapter Twenty-eight

Sid insisted they take her car, but at least she let him drive. It was an SUV, the sort of thing a mother would drive, instead of the flashy car she'd owned when he'd left town, but at least it was a Mercedes. Not that the big engine was doing them any good at the moment.

"This traffic is ridiculous," Joe commented after they'd been on the crowded freeway for a while.

Sid looked up from her digital reader. "The wildfire's caused a lot of roads to be closed. We're stuck with all the rerouted traffic."

Joe was disoriented for a moment, having forgotten that he'd been up in the mountains fighting that fire not long ago.

Sid gave him a quizzical look. "Don't tell me you—"

"Read to me," he cut her off. "We're moving at a snail's pace and I'm bored."

"I'd have to go back to the beginning of the book," she complained.

"My heart bleeds."

"I could arrange that."

He lifted an eyebrow in response. "I'm not afraid, and don't tell me that can be arranged, too."

Sid smiled, and then sighed. "I suppose anything's better than gloomy silence or angry conversation." She backed up the screen, took a deep breath, and read.

"Not again," Zoe muttered as the ship shook from a direct hit once more.

This had been going on far longer than usual, and it was getting worse by the moment. Though her quarters were deep within the center of the command ship's many hulls, she could still feel the energy blows against heavy shielding, and how that shielding was fading. The communications stem in her ear let her know that the whole task force was in trouble and on the run.

* * *

While Joe listened to the story and kept his gaze on the road, a part of his mind roamed, assembling actions, thoughts, scents, psychic impressions, and bits of conversation between Sidonie and himself over the last several days.

"Just how did little Charles come into the world?" he asked after a while.

Sid stopped reading and replied, "Headfirst, like most babies. It was a very easy delivery."

"It wasn't a virgin birth by any chance?"

"I know you know me better than that."

"But you haven't wanted to have sex with anybody in a long time," he said. "Anyone but me, apparently."

"Don't look smug, Bleythin."

"But I'm not a vampire," he went on. "Why am I, lowly werewolf, acceptable, but not one of your own species?"

"Will you stop dissing your own species?" Sid demanded.

"The puzzle is, why are you disrespecting your own species? I have the answer to that," he added.

He didn't want to say it aloud. He wanted to turn the car around and return to San Diego to hunt down and kill any damned Manticore Tribe Prime that had survived the raid on their hideout five years before.

"Some of them took the pledge," she answered

at his emotional reaction. She didn't try to disguise her own bitterness. "They are now learning to be good little vampires under the protection of the Families."

"How can you sound so calm?" His anger was fresh, the pain deep, both for her.

"I've had a few years to practice."

Her emotions roiled, but her tone was cool, her body language and expression almost relaxed. They might as well have been talking about the traffic. Years of practice. Yeah, he could see that.

"You never told me." He hated that he sounded like a hurt little boy. "Or did you, and then made me forget?"

"I never told anyone. I can't tell anyone. I'll never tell anyone. All right?"

"Why?"

"Oh, for goddess's sake, Joe! Think about it! I'm a vampire female," she reminded him. "My mother was a Tribe captive for a long time. Look how she's been treated since she was rescued. I will not allow that to happen to me."

Joe considered, fondly remembered Sid's mom, Lady Antonia Wolf. "She's respected," Joe said. "Beloved. Revered."

"She's treated like she's made out of glass, like a poor little fragile thing that has to be kept in a padded box surrounded by armed guards." Sid laughed. "My esteemed clanfolk ignore the truth about glass, how much heat it can stand, how pliable it can be." She shook her head. "Never mind. What I'm trying to say is that I will not give anyone the chance to treat me like, like—"

"A girl?" he suggested.

"Precisely," she snapped. "Worse than a girl— a *lady*." After an angry silence, she took a deep breath and went on. "You know how hard I've had to fight for what independence I have. Many Clan and Family females think I'm crazy to want a life outside the luxurious confines of the Citadel—they like ruling their own little world and being constantly courted by the Primes."

"That never was your thing," he agreed.

"So, yeah, I got raped," she admitted. "I deliberately put myself in the way of the Manticore Tribe, and I accept what happened."

"It wasn't your fault!"

"Of course not."

She put a hand on his arm. He was surprised at the sexual heat that passed between them, considering the conversation. "Are you really all right?" he asked her.

"No," she answered honestly. "But I am much improved. I will not let having a bad thing happen to me be used to keep me confined and protected. Understood?"

His answer was quick and automatic. "Understood."

He had to remind himself of how badly she'd betrayed him to fight off his own protective urges. He kept his gaze on the crowded highway and his mouth shut.

After a while, she went back to reading to him.

Chapter Twenty-nine

December 18, 2:00 AM
Los Angeles, CA

"Well, here we are. Sort of," Joe said as he parked on a street several blocks away from their destination.

The houses on both sides of the road were dark, their residents peacefully sleeping. Streetlights didn't give much illumination between corners. It was late enough for there to be very little street traffic.

"Sort of," Sid agreed.

A call from Tony along the way had brought them here, instead of their original rendezvous point, his house. Sid got out and stretched as she stood on the sidewalk.

"I wonder what Rose Cameron's disappearance has to do with Dr. Casmerek's clinic?" she asked as Joe came to stand beside her.

"Maybe nothing," Tony Crowe said, stepping from the shadows. "Maybe everything." He glanced between them. "Are you two back together?"

"No," they answered in unison.

"In fact, Joe's going back to his DA buddies now that he's dropped me off," Sid said firmly to Joe.

He shook his head. "No can do, Sidonie."

"Oh, for the love of—!"

"This isn't just to bug you," Joe interrupted the beginning of her irritated tirade. "You said you didn't remember anything, but on the way here you told me that there are reformed Manticore Primes now living among the Families. That's a detail I didn't know, and I was in on the bust. Tobias doesn't know that detail either, does he?"

It was Tony who answered. "When a Tribe Prime leaves his own kind, he becomes a marked man among them. They'll kill him if they can. And reformed bad guys aren't too popular with the Clans or Families until they prove they really, really mean it. So we have our own version of the witness protection program. Hiding rehabilitated Primes is not something anyone among the werefolk would know about."

"Wait a minute, what about Laurent?" Joe asked. "He's a reformed Tribe Prime."

"Laurent's a special case, since he had Mom and me to vouch for him when he came over from the Dark Side," Sid said. "And what about Tobias?" she countered. "Didn't he start out as a Tribe member?"

Joe nodded. "Yeah, but I think he was still a kid when his whole Tribe took the pledge. I'm certain he's not aware that there are Manticores alive he can question. That's a lead you gave us, Sid. There's bound to be more details floating around in your subconscious. I'm staying until you remember everything."

Sid wanted Joe gone—mostly because she wanted him to stay. She was frightened of hurting him even more than she already had. And she was frightened of somehow getting her heart more broken than it already was.

Her sire picked up on her ambiguous reactions. "Life's a bitch, kid," he told her. "No offense," he added to Joe.

"None taken."

"Let the wolf stay," Tony went on. "We can use his nose."

"He isn't here to help with the case," Sid protested.

"I'd be happy to help you find your lady," Joe told Tony.

Sid shot him a stern look. "Are you really in on this case, Bleythin? Or are you just going to get in my way with your Tobias obsession?"

His hand landed on her shoulder, but his firm gaze was on Tony. "I'm in."

How sweet . . . he wanted to help a worried man find his missing loved one. Sid pushed aside her unexpected bitterness but couldn't stop the growl deep in her throat. It was more a werewolf way of expressing frustration than a vampire one, but it perfectly suited her feelings.

Since there was no getting rid of Joe, she concentrated on business. "Why are we meeting here?" she asked Tony.

"Something's happened at the clinic," Joe said. He touched his nose at her annoyed look. "I smell smoke—and explosives."

Fear shot through Sid. "Someone blew up the clinic?"

"Only one room was damaged," Tony said. "I figure it was done as a diversion to keep me from looking for Rose. Everyone else thinks it was an attack from the Purists."

Purists were fanatical remnants of the mortal vampire hunters who loathed the truce between human hunters and their supernatural enemies. Sid hated the very word. *They* were somehow Pure, while she and her kind were somehow *Abominations.*

"Load of crap," she muttered, then got back to business. "The Purists have tried to attack the clinic before, haven't they?"

Tony nodded. "A few years back. We thought we ran them all out of town after that." His eyes went flat and cold. "I still think we did. I think this is something else."

"Something to do with Rose?" Joe asked.

"That's *my* take on it. I think they think that Primes can't multitask."

"Or ask for help when they need it?" Sid added.

Tony gave a humorless laugh. "After all those years on the police force, I know when to form a task force. Rose needs to be found, and my Prime's ego isn't going to be bruised if I don't do all the work myself."

"As long as you're the one who does the actual rescuing," Joe said.

"You've spent too much time around vampires, Lobo," Tony said, but he nodded. "Yeah. You're the detectives. She's the rescuee, I'm the rescuer," he said, defining their roles.

"Unless it works out the other way around," Sid murmured.

Tony gave her a stern look. "Enough talk. I have to get back to the clinic. You know where she was?" he asked.

"Ocean View Retirement Center." She repeated the information he'd given her earlier. "Location already programmed on my GPS."

"I love modern technology." Tony waved them toward her SUV. "What are you waiting for? Go hunt her." Then he was gone.

Joe looked after the Prime with a sour expression. "If he tossed out a stick, would he expect me to fetch it?"

"I think he was ordering *me* around," Sid answered.

She was actually quite pleased at the trust Anthony Crowe was putting in her to accomplish a Prime's work. Most Primes still believed with their whole hearts and testosterone-laden souls that female vampires' roles were limited to child-bearing and ruling empires. Derring-do and ass-kicking were only for the male of the species.

"Except when the Furies are set loose," she added softly.

"The what?"

She repressed a shudder. "You don't want to know." She was going to make certain he *never* knew.

He let it go. "I'm going to ask the question

that needs asking now," he told her. "Keep it professional and don't get all defensive about your sire."

Sid bristled but waited.

"We know that Rose Cameron was a real person."

"Yes?" She drew out the word to several syllables.

"Are you absolutely certain that she is still alive? Are you certain that Tony isn't imagining a relationship with an old movie star?"

"That was two questions," she growled.

Joe nodded and kept looking at her steadily. "And your answers are?"

Sid noticed that her fangs were pressed against her lower lip. It took her a moment, but she managed to sheath her anger and her fangs. She took a deep breath before saying reluctantly, "You're right about that needing to be brought up."

"In an investigation, you have to ask *all* the questions," he reminded her. "You can't take anything—even information from family and friends—at face value."

She nodded and gave another careful moment's thought, going through every remembered conversation. "I've never met Rose, but I've never questioned anything Tony's told me about their relationship. The details certainly seemed realistic. I do not believe that my father is delusional."

"All right, then." Joe sniffed the air. "There's certainly something up around the place Tony guards with his life." He gestured toward the vehicle. "Let's see what we can find out at Rose's last known address."

Chapter Thirty

Joe sat up from being slouched in the passenger seat. Sid glanced his way. He'd been taking a nap until the moment before. His head swiveled slowly from side to side.

"I do not like this," he said.

"L.A. traffic?" Sid wondered. Despite the darkness, the morning rush hour was already under way, or maybe it had never stopped. "Traffic hasn't let up since we left home."

Joe shot her an angry look. "Use all of your senses, Prima," he ordered.

She was tired. It had been a long day. Tony's problem, combined with being near Joe, put her on edge. But none of that was any excuse for falling into the pretense of being mortal. Joe was right and she didn't resent the reminder. She smiled. "Prima?" she asked.

"Concentrate."

"I like the sound of that."

"Then earn it," he growled. He started to unbutton his shirt.

Sid opened her senses, partially to take her mind off the gorgeous body of the werewolf beside her. "Fire on the horizon," she said after a moment.

"How close are we to the nursing home?"

"Exit is coming up."

"Thought it might be." Joe began to take off his trousers.

Sid knew that he was preparing to shape-shift and she had other things to think about, but that didn't stop her from wanting to be distracted. "There's a little old lady in danger," she said.

"Park," Joe said as soon as they were off the exit ramp.

Sid didn't question him, but pulled into the first open space she found, aware of the official mortal hubbub in the distance. Civilians would be blocked from getting anywhere near the emergency area. Better to go in quick and quiet and as their true selves.

The moment she stopped the car, Joe leapt out his side window. Sid watched for a moment as the huge black wolf that was the male she loved raced silently away. She smiled fondly at the shadow moving in the shadows.

What are you waiting for? His thought was flung back at her.

Show-off, she replied, and raced after him. She only had two feet, but she was just as fast and agile as the werewolf.

Joe enjoyed running with Sid, he always had. It was too easy to forget what she'd done to him and fall into their old routine. He made himself a promise to get back to angry later. Right now there was the job, and the excitement of getting past everyone in their way.

The closer they got the more crowded it got. The blaze of the burning building wasn't the only thing lighting the sky, or the only roar of sound. Media helicopters circled overhead, beaming down searchlights. There were news vans parked beyond the cop cars. Fire trucks and EMT vans took up the front row of this circus. Joe was mostly aware of the many mortals on the scene as he wove through pairs of legs. There were hoses and cables to jump over, and, finally, a wall. He knew Sid would make her own silent, swift way through the mess.

Once inside the grounds, Joe waited in the shadow of the wall for his partner to join him. She soon crouched beside him. Her hand touched the back of his neck, fingers stroking through thick fur.

Just like old times.

They watched the building burn and the fire-fighters work. Sparks flew up on a hot wind and the garish flickering light made all the shadows sharp and weird.

"There's nothing alive in there," Sid said. The relief in her voice was soon replaced by annoyance. "Nothing except maybe evidence we need."

Joe nodded his hairy head. *I have no more doubts about your daddy's sanity,* he thought. He rose from his haunches. *I'll have a sniff around anyway.*

And I'll sit here and open my mind to the universe around me.

Have fun with that.

You, too.

Again, it was their usual routine. He made a mental note to add an image of Sid as a telepathic black widow sorting through a web of stolen thoughts and feelings to his catalogue of her evilness. Not that her mental gifts weren't incredibly useful and appreciated on the job.

Chapter Thirty-one

Sid went looking for a witness among the crowd—or even better, the arsonist, here to make sure of his handiwork.

She was initially hit with a wall of mental white noise, the thoughts of all the highly trained professionals going about their jobs. Expecting this, she let herself drift among the consciousnesses of firemen and cops and EMTs. She discovered relief along with puzzlement that there didn't seem to be anyone to rescue inside. *Where are the patients and staff?* she wondered along with the mortals.

As soon as mortal thoughts became the ambient background, she became aware of the vampire. The energy from one of her own kind was a bolt of lightning, a sizzle shot across a blank sky. Sid ignored her natural impulse to contact this other bright awareness. Who was it? What was it doing here? What did it know? She needed a gentle subtle touch here. She began to investigate.

Or she would have, if heavy footsteps hadn't come clumping up to stop beside her. Sid looked up, a long way up, to the sweaty face of a hulking young fireman who was looking worriedly down at her.

Sid groaned at the interruption and rose to her feet.

"May I be of assistance, my lady?" the young Prime asked.

She put a hand on her forehead. "Kiril, isn't it?" she asked.

He grinned at her like a slightly feral puppy. He was one of her own Clan. She hadn't seen him since he'd moved to Los Angeles to become a fireman.

She sighed, but she didn't suspect him of the atrocity blazing behind him. "Kiril Wolfgang."

He put his hand on her elbow, as if she needed support. "I'll get you out of here."

"Ahem," Joe said from behind the shelter of a tree. "The *lady* is already taken care of."

He stepped out in all his naked magnificence.

At least he looked magnificent to Sid; she didn't care what the young Prime's attitude was. Except that he didn't look impressed.

"A werewolf bodyguard is hardly enough protection during such a dangerous time," Kiril told her.

She knew that Joe had meant that she could take care of herself, but she let the Prime's assumptions go.

"What do you mean, *such a dangerous time?*" she demanded. "I know about the attack on the clinic." She gestured toward the fire. "This has something to do with us."

The young Prime nodded his agreement. "I think I felt something supernatural hanging around the perimeter," he said. "Then I spotted you and came for a look."

"There're more than two vampires in the vicinity," Joe said. "At least there were."

"Can you pick up a trail?" Sid asked.

"I want to hear what else our friend has to say," he answered. "There's a lot going on."

Kiril nodded. "The bar downtown took a hit earlier, made to look like a drive-by. A car bomb went off outside Shaggy Harker's bike shop. A supposed stalker tried to attack the movie star who's really a Prime."

"Werefolk as well as vampires are being targeted?" Sid asked. Shaggy was alpha of the local werewolf pack.

"There's a vampire movie star?" Joe asked.

They glanced at each other and smiled at the way they'd asked each other's natural question.

Kiril nodded to both questions. "It's not safe for you to be out here, Lady Sidonie. I have to get you back to the Shagal Citadel right now."

Despite the various Clan and Family members who dwelled in the area, Los Angeles was the home territory of the Shagal Clan—the Jackals. Lady Serisa Shagal was Matri of this Clan, and her word was law here, the way Lady Juanita Wolf's was among all vampires in San Diego. Kiril naturally assumed that any female vampire would be a guest at the Shagal Citadel, as it was the safest place in the city and the girls had to be kept safe.

Sid didn't argue with him. "Joe and I will make our own way back to the Citadel," she told the Wolf Prime, using a commanding tone and attitude that reminded the kid that he was a Wolf and not a Jackal. "You have your own work to do here."

It got him off her case. "Watch her closely," he commanded the werewolf.

"Oh, I will," Joe drawled.

"Irony is lost on our young Kiril," Sid said

as she watched him head back to his firefighting duties. She was surprised when Kiril turned back and gave her a sheepish look.

"I'm sorry I couldn't make it home for your Severing ceremony," he said. "I know how important that is, especially the first time. Belated congratulations on your son's beginning his journey, Lady Sidonie."

For a moment all Sid could do was stare blankly, then she forced a smile. "Thank you."

He grinned and was off.

So was Joe.

"Where are you going?" she asked Joe when he shifted back to wolf form and headed away from the disaster area. She followed him all the way back to the SUV; he was in human shape by the time she reached him. He was sitting inside the vehicle but he wasn't pulling on his clothes. Instead he was talking on his cellular phone. Sid got behind the wheel and shamelessly listened in on Joe's conversation.

"They aren't going to like that," she said when he flipped the phone shut.

"Do I care?" he asked. "Do you?"

She shook her head. "My pride's not on the line. Anything that doesn't specifically affect finding Rose Cameron isn't on my agenda."

"I didn't think you'd mind."

She glanced at the glow in the sky and worried about an old lady. "Where to now?"

Joe patted her ever-so-gently on the shoulder. "I'm under orders to get you safely to the Citadel."

She flashed fangs at him but trusted that he had a reason and started the engine.

Chapter Thirty-two

December 18, 5:00 AM

"You're doing a recon," Sid realized as Joe accompanied her into the thoroughly modern mansion that was the Shagal Citadel.

He gave her a conspiratorial smile and put his finger over his lips.

It's not like you're going into hostile territory, she thought to him.

Yet, he replied.

After that, they observed mental silence while they were led to the Citadel's windowless central room. Rather, she was politely led and Joe came along in her wake, pretty much unnoticed by the vampires around them. Just the way he wanted it.

It took an effort for Sid to hide her amusement at the arrogance of her own kind.

She'd expected to find a crowd of worried vampires holding a conference in the meeting room and was surprised to find the only occupant was a female with a wireless e-reader perched on her lap.

The female vampire looked up irritably at the interruption, then a slow smile spread across her face. She was looking at Joe.

Sid barely managed not to snarl or possessively step in front of Joe to block the female's view. "Hello, Flare," she said to Francesca "Flare" Reynard. "What are you doing in town?" she added suspiciously. "I thought you'd moved back to Idaho."

"I did." Flare languidly rose to her feet out of a deeply cushioned leather chair.

All vampires were attractive, but black-haired and vividly pale Flare Reynard made other vampire females look like warty frogs in comparison. Despite her haughtiness, her temper, and her goddess looks, Sid liked her. She and Flare had shared an apartment in college, living a few years completely among mortals. They also shared a lot of the same dissatisfaction with their lot in life, but they reacted differently. Whereas Sid was sneaky and diplomatic and tried to stay under the radar to do what she wanted, Flare raged and ranted and rebelled. She still ended up obeying her Matri, under protest, in matters regarding the survival of the Fox Clan.

"Why are you in Los Angeles?" Sid asked Flare.

"I've got an appointment to get pregnant. You've started a trend, girlfriend." She gave a sharp laugh. "What does it say about our species, when the males prefer mortals and the females prefer a turkey baster?"

"It doesn't say anything," Sid answered. "Except that you need to take love where you find it, and that a couple of us are trying to preserve our species using modern science. Were you at the clinic when it was bombed?" she asked, suddenly worried about Flare's future offspring.

Flare nodded. "I'd just finished having some tests when the little bitty boom went off. Now I'm going to wait for an all-clear to sound before I can get knocked up.

"I wanted to stay at the clinic and help, but here I am. After all, it wasn't much of a bomb."

"It was enough to get the mortals' attention," a deep male voice said from the doorway.

"That was the point, I suppose," Flare added as they all turned to the Shagal Elder, Barak. "Now I'm stuck here for the duration."

"For your own safety, Lady Francesca," Barak said patiently, ignoring her ungracious attitude. "Welcome, Lady Sidonie, young werewolf," he added with a nod to her and Joe.

Sid couldn't help but smile appreciatively. The tall, dark-skinned Prime had a beautiful deep voice, and the gray in his black hair only added to his charm. He and Matri Serisa had been bonded for at least a hundred years. *Lucky woman*, Sid thought.

She introduced Joe, who said, "It's an honor to meet you, sir."

After the introductions, Barak went on. "I am told you are the finest telepath of your Clan, Lady Sidonie."

Sid couldn't look at Joe, knowing this reminded him of her betrayal. "Thank you," she managed.

"We could use your help dealing with too much mortal attention," Barak went on. "It seems that today's attacks were deliberately staged to reveal our existence, and now we're fighting to stay in hiding. We'd appreciate your adding your telepathic skills to rearrange mortal perceptions."

"I can help with that," Flare said.

Barak looked her over gravely. "That would not be wise, Lady Francesca. Your Matri would not wish it."

Flare flounced back to her chair, picked up her reader, and pretended they weren't there.

Though Sid was on a missing person case, she could continue that hunt while rearranging mortal minds. She'd been settling into a telepathic hunt when Kiril interrupted her, and there might be mortal perps involved in today's crime scenes. Those perps might lead them to Rose Cameron.

"I'd be happy to help," she told Barak. "Excuse me a moment," she added, and took Joe aside. "What'll you be up to while I'm messing with minds?" she asked her partner.

I'll finish the recon of the Citadel first," he said. "Then I'll go back to the remains of the nursing home and sniff around."

"Think you'll find anything?"

"No. But lack of evidence might also tell us something."

She didn't know what he meant but trusted his instincts. "Good hunting."

She resisted the impulse to give him a quick kiss.

Chapter Thirty-three

Joe certainly couldn't fault the vampires' security setup. Everything—cameras, motion detectors, alarm systems, panic room—was state of the art. And there were plenty of Prime guards on the grounds and in the house, unobtrusive but on full alert. No one was going to cause trouble at the Shagal Citadel. The bad guys had known not to bother trying, at least not until they were able to drain more defenders away from the place. Joe still noted every detail of the inside setup and automatically filed it away.

But as hard as he tried, he couldn't keep his mind completely on business.

Damn it, Sid, what is going on? With you? With me? Us?

With Charles?

He'd found out from Sid and Flare's conversation that Charles had been conceived by artificial means. That didn't sound like vampires. Vampires were the randiest creatures on the planet. Locker room talk had it that the females were even more sexually active than the Primes. Back in the day, didn't the females used to keep whole harems of satisfied Primes? It would be easier to understand if Sid's baby was the result of an orgy. Vampires were supposed to do that sort of thing. It was normal, healthy activity for their species.

What was Sid up to? What did she want?

Did it have anything to do with him?

Why would it?

What was he missing? And why did he care?

The confusion and questions clawed at him. It took an effort to keep his thoughts and emotions shielded. He didn't want to add to the psychic static the vampire telepaths were already working through. And he sure as hell didn't want to draw Sid's finely honed telepathic attention to his questions. To his—all right to his anguish. The melodrama was embarrassing, but his pain was real.

Damn the woman, anyway.

Not a woman. A vampire female. Too high above me or anybody bloody else to—

"But you said . . ." Joe stopped and closed his eyes.

Five Years Ago

"I love you, but I can't recall anyone ever kissing my knee before. It tickles," Sid said.

"I love this knee," he said between kisses. "I could write poetry to this knee."

" 'An Ode to a Joint'?" She laughed. "Sounds like drug humor."

Joe looked up the length of Sid's naked body and fully appreciated the way her bare breasts moved with her laughter. " 'A Poem to a Patella'" he said. "And a sonnet to your thighs," he added as he moved farther up the inside of her legs.

Her laughter turned into a breathy, needy whimper. She raised her hips; fingers tangled in his hair. "Joseph, if you stop short of where I want you to go, I'll die."

"I won't allow that," he told her. Their gazes met on his promise. "I'll never allow that."

"And I'll do the same for you."

The whole universe became suddenly . . . quiet.

Heavy. Waiting. He knew with his whole being that this moment was important. There was no one but them, and being together meant every-thing.

"I love you," he said.

"I love you," she answered.

The universe began to spin again, and it was filled with brightness and joy. She smiled and held her arms out to him. Her smile was everything. Holding her was everything. Making love with her was more than everything.

"Be with me forever," he said.

But Sid didn't answer.

Present Day

Joe ran a hand over his head and absently noted that he'd spent enough time in wolf form for the buzz cut to have grown out, a residual effect of the transformation. It was hard for a werewolf to wear short hair. Their natural tendency was to-ward long, heavy locks, the sort females liked to run their fingers through.

Sid certainly liked playing with his hair.

He smiled bitterly. Maybe that was the reason she'd spent a long weekend using him as her boy toy. Maybe Primes were too neat and tidy for her taste.

What are you doing, standing here feeling sorry for yourself, Bleythin? Your community is under attack, and there's a fragile mortal who's missing. Get on with the hunt!

The hunt for Rose Cameron would take all his attention. The hunt would keep him sane.

Besides, he'd told his partner he was returning to the burned out building and when it came to business, they trusted each other to do what they said.

Chapter Thirty-four

December 18, 1944, 7:00 PM
Ardennes Forest, Belgium

The reek of congealing blood bothered Tony more than the sight of the two bodies he'd pulled out of the foxhole. The GIs had gone to their maker. He'd make sure at least two of the enemy died to avenge them, but there was nothing he could do for the corpses. What the smell of their blood was doing to him, on the other hand, was—

"Are you going to be sick?" Rose asked.

He was, but not in any way he could explain. What he did was move closer to her and breathe in the sweet awareness of her life. Her heartbeat, her blood flowed, her thoughts were bright points of light. He reveled in her warmth when her hand unexpectedly touched his cheek.

"Because if you're going to be sick," Rose went on, "I'll join you. Not that I think of vomiting as a communal sort of activity . . . but in wartime . . ."

"It's not really possible to lighten the mood in the middle of a battlefield." He put his hand over hers. "But thanks for trying."

"I'm with the USO. It's my duty to improve morale," she reminded him.

"Your very existence improves my morale." He helped her into the shallow protection of the foxhole before kneeling up to peer around the dark woods. It was snowing again. "It's quiet."

"Too quiet?" she whispered. When he gave her a sardonic look, she added, "You're a scout. You need to find out about enemy troop movements, don't you?"

His conscience pained him, torn between his assignment and Rose's safety. "I—"

"Go do your job," she ordered. "I'll wait here. I'll be fine."

"All right," he said after a moment. "Don't you dare go anywhere."

* * *

December 18, 1:00 PM
Present Day
Los Angeles, CA

Of course, Rose hadn't been where he'd left her when he returned back then, either, Tony recalled.

"Can't you ever stay put?" he complained to his missing love as he parked several blocks up the street from the burned-out ruin of Rose's last known whereabouts. The place he had thought so safe for her was now a smoking ruin. His only comfort was in knowing that she hadn't been there when the place was destroyed.

And the other residents? his mortal-protecting conscience questioned. That was one of the things he was here to check.

The acrid scent of smoke lingered in the air, heavy enough to make Tony's throat ache. He approached carefully, moving with the silent speed that to mortal eyes seemed like a passing cloud's shadow or a moment's dizziness.

Stealth was required, as the place was far from deserted. Forensic techs and arson investigators moved through the soaked, charred ruins and smashed garden. He knew from experience that firemen intent on putting out blazes necessarily ran roughshod over any potential crime scene evidence. This always frustrated him when he was a police detective, but it wasn't his problem this time. It was supernatural evidence he needed now. To find it, he went searching for a large black wolf.

"Well?" he asked Joe when he came across the werewolf, who had his nose to the ground at the back wall of the property.

The wolf rounded on him with a snarl, then blinked very unwolflike blue eyes in recognition. Joe moved behind an undamaged hibiscus bush and morphed into his human shape.

"Why do vampires always have to make an entrance?" he asked when Tony joined him.

Tony rubbed the back of his neck. "Personally, I blame Bram Stoker. Well?" he repeated.

"I need to talk to Tobias," Joe answered.

Tony quivered with leashed fury. "You're working for *me* today."

"Your situation is only part of the problem."

It took far more effort than normal not to rip the youngster to shreds. If Joe hadn't been the love of his daughter's life, he might have killed him then and there. Then again, disposing of Joe might be the best thing he could do for her . . .

Tony moved closer to the werewolf.

He saw that Joe recognized the danger, but

he didn't back down. He locked gazes with Tony and they looked at each other steadily until Tony calmed down.

Eventually, Tony nodded. "What can you tell me?"

Joe gestured toward the ruins. "There weren't any mortals in there and hadn't been for at least four hours before the fire was set. There are dozens of mortal scent trails leading away from the place. I need to plot out a map and check them all out."

"Only mortal scent trails?"

Joe shrugged. "Werefolk can cover their scent tracks these days. And you know how vampire telepathy makes it hard for us to track you."

Tony nodded. "Anything else?"

"Roses," Joe answered. "An overpowering scent of roses."

The image summoned by those words twisted Tony's heart and his gut. Color and scent and memory overwhelmed him.

"That's my doing," he croaked through the constricting pain in his throat. "I send dozens of them to her every year. I called her my 'Rose in winter,' and—"

He turned away for a moment, overcome by the worry and fear that choked him.

"Don't blame yourself," Joe said.

Tony turned back to the youngster. "I most certainly do *not* blame myself. Not for all the years we should have been together, or for her disappearance. I do blame myself for leaving her alone. I shouldn't have done that."

"Her kidnapping wasn't something you could have seen coming." Joe gestured at the charred rubble. "You couldn't have expected that."

"I will kill the bastard that's responsible, whether Rose is harmed or not." And Anthony Crowe always kept his vows.

"Good for you. But the roses—"

"The roses I'd sent her were gone yesterday. Her room was completely empty."

His pain eased at Joe's sudden grin. "Maybe they took the roses with her. I can follow the roses."

Tony was eager to let him. But duty called. "Will the scent last for a few more hours?"

"Certainly, but—"

"You're wanted back at the Citadel. Put on some fur and let's go."

Chapter Thirty-five

Tony sat with every appearance of patience behind the wheel while Joe finished putting on the jeans and shirt he'd found folded on the passenger seat. Joe was amazed at what a fine actor the Prime was, because he could sense that Tony was not nearly as calm and collected as he appeared. Oh, Tony's psychic senses were well shielded, but being this close, the werewolf was very aware of chemical signs of agitation that were impossible for anyone to mask. Except—

There was this wonderful perfume Sid always wore . . .

Joe bit back a curse, and forced his thoughts away from Sidonie Wolf.

"Am I in trouble with the powers that be?" Joe asked.

"The powers that be wouldn't tell me if you were."

Joe knew very well that Tony Crowe was a trusted senior Prime of this territory, even if he wasn't officially a member of the Shagal Clan. Joe guessed the reason that Tony didn't live among his own Corvus Clan had something to do with Rose Cameron.

Joe had always thought he knew about vampires, but he guessed you had to be whelped and raised in a culture to completely understand it. It was clear that Tony had secrets, and issues with his own kind. As did Sidonie—who he was trying not to think about.

"Why did Sid have Charles the way she did?" he asked.

This got him a blistering look from Sidonie's sire. "And where has my daughter's best friend been the last three years?" he questioned in turn.

Joe worked hard to hold on to his temper. "You do know that she screwed me over, don't you?"

"I do."

"Do you know why?"

"Not my story to tell, even if I do."

This reminded Joe of how Sid kept her sire's

secrets. Joe admired both vampires for their loyalty to each other, but . . .

"She's no angel, that daughter of yours."

Tony gave an ironic smile. "I should say not."

Joe hated that he agreed with Tony's jovial tone. Then again, why not accept Sidonie for who she was, even if he didn't completely know her?

Unable to let his curiosity go, Joe tried for politeness this time. "Can I ask another question about Sid and Charles?"

"No."

"What's a Severing ceremony?" he asked anyway.

Tony gave him a sharp look. "How do you know about that?"

"Sid's reacting strangely whenever her son is mentioned, and I'm beginning to suspect I know why."

"You don't need to know. It's not important."

Joe took a long, deep breath. "The change in your scent says it is. Give me a break and let her partner in on this," he appealed to the retired cop. "She isn't at a hundred percent, and I think I need to know why."

"I don't see why you need to know secret vampire stuff."

"If I'm kept in the dark, I might say something

ignorant at the wrong time that could jeopardize Sid, me, and our client."

"Your client being my Rose?"

"Precisely."

Tony frowned as he drove in silence for a few minutes. Joe waited, so anxious to discover what was wrong with Sid that he ached. He shouldn't be aching with worry for her, but . . .

"There was a time when our females never left the safety of the Clan citadels. They kept harems, but they lived in purdah," Tony eventually said.

Joe knew some of the history of vampire feminism from Sid, but he kept quiet, wanting to find out what Tony was building up to.

"We thought we were keeping them safe, but when vampire hunters made a concentrated effort to attack the citadels, we almost lost our females. No females, no vampires. The females decided that they were in just as much danger whether they lived in seclusion or not, and they've gradually been coming out into the world. This is all very well and good for them on a personal level, but there is the slight problem of maternal instinct that needs to be addressed if they are going to have their freedom." Tony glanced at Joe. "Are you following this, wereboy?"

Joe shook his head. "We raise our young in the pack. It takes a pack to raise a cub."

It was an old but true saying. Even with the camaraderie of the DA, Joe deeply missed contact with his own people. And whose fault was that? Could he really blame Sid for his choices?

"I wish vampires could do it that way. Maybe we did once upon a time, when we lived in the mythical hidden cities and didn't spend so much of our time among mortals. Since we don't live in the past, we have to adjust to survive. Our females wanted—and needed—more freedom," he added reluctantly. "But one of the costs of this freedom was having to tone down the strongest maternal instinct of any species on the planet. Our female children don't give us any problems until they reach puberty. Much like teenage girls everywhere," he added with a chuckle. "But around two, our little boys quite literally turn into animals and need constant supervision."

"I know about the crèches . . . but . . . I take it they aren't exclusive private schools for young Primes, as we're led to believe?"

Tony snorted. "The crèches are where we protect, civilize, and educate our boys. To save our species we have to channel the boys' aggression, but our females don't take well to being separated from their babies."

"So you have a Severing ceremony when the kids are old enough to be separated from their mothers?"

"Precisely."

Tony seemed to think this was explanation enough, and silence ensued for a few minutes.

"And?" Joe finally prodded.

"And . . ." He sighed "We telepathically mess with the mamas' heads so that they don't go completely insane when their babies are taken away. It's for the best."

Joe noted that Tony didn't seem completely convinced of that, and he was dumbfounded himself. Werewolf parents would *never* be separated from their babies.

"Vampire females voluntarily allow their memories to be subverted?" he questioned.

"Of course not!" Tony answered. "They're the best mothers in the world, the most fiercely protective. They instinctively cannot be separated from their children. The Severing was a compromise the Matri Council came up with to bring their daughters into the nineteenth century, and it still works for the Clans. Without the Severing our females would have to return to living in purdah, but it's better to live in the modern world. So, we block the pain."

"It's barbaric!"

Tony seemed almost amused by Joe's outrage. "We're vampires."

"Have you heard of the concept of free will?"

Tony nodded. "I have. And it's all very well for mortals, but we don't always have the luxury of doing exactly as we please. Survival of the species has to take precedence over individual rights sometimes. As it is, Sidonie will be separated from her son for a few years, but the killing pain of the separation will be blunted. It was done for her own good, and you will keep your mouth shut about it. Won't you?"

The question was asked in such an unmistakably dangerous tone that Joe had no doubt his life was being threatened.

Joe wouldn't let himself be intimidated, but he now had too much to think about to push it any further. "I'll keep it to myself."

At least for now.

Chapter Thirty-six

The blue-eyed black wolf ran through her thoughts, but there was nothing unusual in that. Even with years of practice, it wasn't easy for Sid to block the awareness of Joe. It didn't help that he was nearby. Or that his thoughts kept turning to her. Or that they'd been together and made love—

Had sex.

Call it what she would, the visceral memory of their bodies moving together got in the way of her mental control. Joe pressed against her consciousness, made it hard to send her thoughts anywhere but toward him.

I was able to do this last night, Sid reminded

herself. *What did I do to—oh, yes, I was too worried about Rose to dwell on my own stupid problems. Rose it is, then.*

Rose? Where are you? You don't know me, but I am a friend. Tony told me that you are telepathic, that you could at least communicate with him. You can talk to me. I'm a friend. I'm his friend. Don't be frightened.

An analytical part of Sid's awareness separated from the psychic search. Of course Rose was afraid—or had she just sensed fear?

Do you know where you are, Rose? Show me what you see.

Sid cleared her mind of every thought, every image. She floated in darkness, alone. After a while there was no floating, no self. Only darkness.

Pink.

A thin pink ribbon swirled in the blackness. Sid stretched out to meet the color.

Yellow wound around the pink. Small explosions of white and scarlet lit the blackness. Crystal carved, cold as ice. Green.

Everything settled onto a painless bed of green.

"I hate to disturb you."

Weight returned. Heartbeat. Breathing. Sid opened her eyes to blotches of white, black, and emerald green. After a moment, she recognized that the blotches made up a pattern. That the pattern was a face. The green spots were eyes. The eyes looked worriedly into hers.

"Flare Reynard."

"You don't sound very sure of that," Flare said. Her bright laughter was as sharp as the crystal. She touched a fingertip to Sid's cheek. "Cold as ice. How deep in were you?"

It took a while for these words to sink in, longer for them to make sense. "How deep? Into someone else's head." She took a shaky breath. "I'm not sure where I was or what was going on. I sensed colors, and maybe . . ." Sid shook her head. "Whatever I was picking up was totally useless."

She became aware that she was seated in a brocade-upholstered chair in one of the Shagal Citadel's guest bedrooms.

Sid looked blankly at Flare. "How long have I been out?"

"You said you wanted to meditate before trying to reach out and touch any witnesses," Flare said to fill her in. "That was four hours ago."

All that time and psychic energy expended with so little to show for it? Sid was disgusted. So much for being the best telepath of her Clan. She could only hope that she'd picked up some details that she wasn't consciously aware of. She knew better than to try to force anything to the surface.

Something to do with Rose would pop up, or it wouldn't.

It finally occurred to her to wonder why Flare had interrupted her. "This isn't a social call, is it?"

"Oh, no," Flare answered with a sly smile. There was a glint of excitement in her emerald eyes. "There's finally a bit of excitement going on around here."

Sid wondered at Flare's definition of excitement. "Something more exciting than every supernatural enclave in town being attacked?"

"All right, let's say something I find more interesting is going on."

Flare went to a small table across the room and came back to Sid with a small cup cradled in her palms. Sid sat up straight, catching the warm scent as Flare approached.

Flare made a formal bow as she handed Sid the cup. "With Lady Serisa's compliments."

Sid stood to accept the gift. The lotus-shaped cup was of alabaster, so finely carved it was translucent. It held no more than a thimbleful of fresh mortal blood. Sid held it cupped in her hands as Flare had done, absorbing the warmth through her palms. She breathed in the aroma, savored the rich scarlet color. Her heart raced and the tang of anticipation filled her mouth and throat.

"Matri Serisa does me great honor." The words were ritual but completely heartfelt. She lifted the cup to her lips.

One drop on her tongue sent all her senses into overdrive. Sid had to sit down quickly, careful not to spill any of the precious liquid.

"Forgot the rush, didn't you?" Flare asked.

Sid looked up at her friend over the edge of the cup. "It has been a long time." She took another drop on her tongue.

The world was a sharper, more vivid place, and she was the most alive thing in it.

"Stop looking so orgasmic, girl—you're making me jealous."

"That's not orgasmic, that's just invigorated. I hadn't realized how tired I was."

Flare nodded. "Sometimes we forget that this is our natural nourishment."

Sid took a deeper sip. She could taste the ancient mixture of herbs blended into the blood that helped keep the substance from becoming a consuming addiction. She didn't know who had discovered the herbal recipe thousands of years before, but the mixture had been the vampires' first step toward civilization. It had been the first step toward living with mortals as kindred, instead of using other sentient beings as cattle. These days, almost any properly processed mammalian blood could be used for sustenance. The blood of mortals was taken as an erotic sharing with willing mortal lovers. Or, like now, a ritual tasting offered from an anonymous volunteer.

But Sid was long past the point where she could appreciate more than a few bracing sips of mortal blood.

She handed the still-warm cup back to Flare. "With my compliments."

Flare's perfect brows arched in surprise. "Are you sure you don't want this?"

"I prefer werewolf." Sid clapped a hand over her mouth, but the words were already out. The blood must have made her drunk to loosen her tongue so easily. "Oh, crap!"

Flare's eyes sparkled with interest. "I'm in love with a mortal, and you're involved with a werewolf? I think you and I have a lot of catching up to do." She tossed down the rest of the blood. "But right now, we're wanted at the meeting."

Sid was so grateful for the distraction that she followed Flare without asking any questions. A crowd of vampires, werefolk, and mortals filled the huge central room. Hostility was thick in the air, most of it aimed at the big Prime standing boldly in the center of the meeting space. Tobias

Strahan was the sort who naturally drew attention to himself, but Sid's gaze went instantly to the werewolf standing beside Tobias.

The sight of him made her heart ache and sing, but she never got tired of looking at her Joe.

Chapter Thirty-seven

December 1944
Belgium

"*When was the last time you slept?*" Rose asked Anthony.

He ran a hand over his unshaven face. "*I don't need a lot of sleep.*"

"*You look terrible.*"

Artillery fire interrupted their conversation and they flattened themselves at the bottom of the foxhole. The trees behind them and the snow piled up in front would be inadequate protection if firing was turned their way. Somehow, though, Rose felt safe with Anthony's arms around her. He was the only warm thing in this frigid hell. The darkness was lit with explosions; the noise was deafening.

"It makes me want to scream," Rose whispered in Anthony's ear.

"Nah, you're not the panicking type," he whispered back.

Or were they whispering? When she spoke like this, she wasn't aware of her lips moving.

"If we get out of this I intend to have a good, long panic."

"We're close to the crossroads town I told you about. Once we get there, you'll be safe."

He rose on his knees to take a look around.

"Crossroads town?" she asked when he ducked back down.

"Bastogne," he reminded her, and helped her to her feet.

Present Day

Well, wasn't that just jumping from the frying pan into the fire? An hour after we got to Bastogne, the town was surrounded by the Germans.

Wait—aren't I supposed to be dead? Then why am I dreaming? And thinking?

"She looks so peaceful."

"I've always thought she was lovely."

And hearing.

Two voices, one familiar. Her Russian nurse, Gregor, had just said she was lovely. Rose had no idea who'd said she looked peaceful. Her undertaker? No. She wasn't dead. She couldn't move, but she was aware that she was breathing, and not in any ragged, soon-to-be-her-last-breath way, either. Damn.

Rose remembered getting up to get the stash of pills, but after that—

"Once I let one of my females take my blood. It was much more fun than this."

Rose wondered what Gregor meant by that.

"Are you planning on draining me dry?" he demanded.

The edge in his voice frightened her, but the other man responded coolly, "You told me to take as much as I needed. Since you insist on leaving, I'm taking as much as I safely can. We have a bargain, if you recall."

"We've donated to you for years."

"Ours has been a symbiotic relationship with a parasitic life form. Your blood in exchange for our perfecting the Dawn drug for you has been a far more enlightened policy than our ancestors' attempts at killing one another."

"You've been behaving in a civilized manner because you discovered that we're easier to capture than we are to keep."

"That was an unfortunate scenario. It almost ruined the whole project."

"It almost destroyed everything," Gregor said. "Now my sponsors think you've experimented enough. They see the current results as the success they promised you."

"Your sponsors are wrong. The experiment is still at a very delicate stage."

"I agree. Which is why I am going to explain this to them in person."

The other man chuckled. "Heads will literally roll, I trust?"

"That would be pleasant," Gregor answered.

"How long will this take?" The other man seemed worried. "Your presence will be required if the results prove unstable."

"You don't need *me* specifically," Gregor countered. "I am making arrangements for a replacement."

"Ah, good. There. I'm finished. Would you care for a drink?"

There was something unpleasant about the question, and Gregor's answering laugh made Rose's skin crawl. It made her want to cover her ears and run away.

But she wasn't sure she even had ears. She certainly couldn't run. She was floating in a gray limbo, disembodied—frightened.

Where was Anthony? She'd gotten used to living her life alone, but she couldn't stand it anymore. Where was he when she needed him?

The same place he always was—in her dreams. All she could do was pray for the dreams to rise up out of the darkness and rescue her.

All she got was the darkness.

Chapter Thirty-eight

$\mathcal{M}$usic brought Rose up out of the darkness. Not music playing on a radio somewhere, though. It took a while for her to realize that the song was playing in her head. One she didn't know but must have heard somewhere. It was about bitterness and forgiveness and taking responsibility in a relationship and—it was by that Irish band, wasn't it?

Or maybe it was about religion, because the line about raising the dead kept repeating over and over, and her annoyance with it finally brought her fully awake.

Rose was afraid to open her eyes. She'd thought she'd stopped being afraid of anything a long time ago, but she knew that there was something so wrong that she couldn't bear to face it.

Coward.

She thought for a moment that the voice in her head might be Anthony's, but when the moment passed, she was all too aware that she was completely alone and talking to herself.

Coward.

And what's wrong with being a coward occasionally?

It would seem that coherent thought had returned. Rose sighed, becoming aware of her breathing and that there was something different about it. What was it?

She concentrated on the simple action of air entering and exiting her lungs. It happened far too easily. The contours of her body against the mattress felt different as well. The constant numb coldness was also absent from her hands and feet. Her body felt solid and real, but—wrong.

The wrongness frightened her, and the fear permeated her, body, mind, and soul.

Are you going to let a little thing like utter terror get you down?

Rose took a deep breath, a far deeper breath than she'd managed in years, and resolutely opened her eyes.

She saw—her room? She hadn't expected that.

And she was still surrounded by roses. She had been breathing in their scent, and maybe that was what had kept her from total, screaming panic. Was being scared spitless better than total panic? She wished that Anthony was present for her to consult on the subject.

She frowned at her own neediness.

Maybe it would have been better if he hadn't come back into her life if it meant she was going to go all soft and girlish after a lifetime of taking care of herself.

And was it possible to be girlish with varicose veins, osteoporosis, and all the other indignities life visited upon one?

It was possible to be foolish at any age, Rose decided, but all pretension to girlishness had gone long ago.

"And good riddance."

Stop stalling. There's something wrong. Find out what.

Why? She demanded of that practical, curious, braver side of herself. *Maybe I'll just ring for an aide to bring me a cup of tea.*

That will only be pretending that nothing is wrong. It'll only forestall the inevitable. Why bother?

All right. Fine.

Rose sat up, then stared straight ahead and

tried to figure out why sitting up was such a strange experience.

There were pictures on the wall opposite her: a small van Gogh that was *not* a reproduction, and three framed photographs of people dear to her. She could see each picture quite clearly. And wasn't the wall a brighter shade of beige than yesterday, with more pink in the creamy tone than she had ever noticed before?

What on earth was the matter with her eyes?

Not a thing.

She knew that was the answer, but it didn't make any sense. And the reason that sitting up had felt wrong was because she hadn't felt anything.

"No—"

She clapped a hand over her mouth, afraid that saying it would make it true. Or only prove that she was insane. Maybe she was crazy. Or maybe she was dead. Either state would make more sense than what she was feeling. Which was nothing.

"No pain. There is no pain."

Even after she made herself speak this blatant falsehood aloud it remained true. And she could see better because—her vision was clear. Cataract surgery a few years ago hadn't been able to completely restore her age-dimmed sight, but the clarity was there now.

She knew what was wrong: she felt great! She felt—no, she wasn't going to think the word.

Rose looked at her hands. She recognized them all right, but as a distant memory, not the thin, age-spotted claws Anthony had held so tenderly on his visit. She threw back the covers and slid her legs over the side of the bed. With no difficulty.

"Betty Grable, eat your heart out," Rose murmured when she got a look at her gams.

Though she supposed Uma Thurman would be the closest comparison among modern actresses. If that young woman were a tall, skinny, freckled redhead who happened to have the right bone structure to be loved by the camera.

She stood. She meant to do it slowly, and carefully, but it was easier to spring out of the bed. Instinct seemed to have taken over from the awareness that quick movement could break fragile bones. She flexed her bare toes, reveling in the sensual feel of the thick pile of the Persian rug beneath her feet. How was it that everything felt so wonderful, so new?

Rose tentatively ran her hands up and down the length of her body, then looked down the neck of her nightgown.

"Good Lord almighty."

There was a full-length mirror on the closet

door. It was the hardest thing Rose had ever done to turn around and look at herself. Even harder than walking away from Anthony. But . . .

The young woman in the mirror looked just like that young woman in Paris in 1944.

"That is the most ridiculous thing I have ever seen." Although she was in deep shock, her voice was calm. And it was a young woman's voice.

"You are beautiful."

She turned to face Gregor, who was standing in the doorway. "I am an abomination," she told him. "And *you* are a vampire."

Chapter Thirty-nine

"You're very observant, Rose."

"Then why haven't I noticed before?"

"You've noticed several times in the last year," he said as he shut the door behind him. "Before today, I've always had to make you forget."

For a moment Rose's reaction was relief that she hadn't gone completely senile, then anger exploded through her. "You've been messing with my mind?"

"Among other things."

It was the sort of smug answer a stupid question like that deserved, and Rose calmed down. She was still shaking with shock and fear, but now she was determined not to let any emotion get the better of her.

"You might want to sit down," Gregor suggested. "You look like you're about to fall."

Rose sneered. "Ever the helpful nurse, aren't you?"

He tsked. "You were such a sweet little old lady." Gregor picked her up by the waist and deposited her in the nearest chair, then took a seat on the bed. After he glanced at his watch he said, "I have some time to kill and you're dying of curiosity. Ask me anything you like."

"What happened to your Russian accent?"

"It's still there," he answered, "but I practice speaking American when I have to deal with the outside world. Which I must leave to do in a few minutes, so let us have a meaningful conversation in the time we have left, dear Rose."

That he called her *dear* grated, but she let it go. "What's a Tribe vampire doing out in the daylight?"

Gregor smiled affectionately. "You noticed that I am sitting in the patch of sunlight from your window. Of course, if you look outside you will notice that your view has changed significantly. We kept the room the same to help you remain calm while still in the test environment."

"Anything to keep the lab rat happy?"

"Precisely."

"Tribe bastard."

"And you infer that I am Tribe because—"

"No Clan or Family Prime would kidnap someone and do this to them!"

He laughed. "Do what? Make a dying crone young and beautiful again? How is that a crime? But you guess correctly; I am Tribe." He leaned forward and touched the tip of her nose. Rose managed not to flinch, but just barely. "Your Anthony told you far too much about vampires."

"Knowledge I was perfectly willing to take to my grave."

"Oh, you still will." His tone was cheerful, but the look in his green eyes was chilling.

"You were such a sweet nurse," she said. "I don't suppose you actually are a nurse, are you?"

"Tribe Primes do not pursue humanitarian careers. I did not participate in this rejuvenation experiment out of the goodness of my heart." He looked her over in a thorough, intimate way that made Rose blush. "Mortals are commodities. Some make good pets for a time, some prove inconvenient, but all are disposable animals." He smiled, showing quite a bit of fang, and she didn't recognize him at all. He added, "And you are all delicious."

She flexed her young fingers, rubbed the firm flesh of her arms, touched the soft red curls framing her flawless face. "If mortals are disposable animals, why perform an experiment to make a mortal more like a vampire? What do you get out of it?"

His smile this time was one of genuine delight. "Those are excellent questions. Thank you, Rose Cameron, for realizing that what we have done to you was for the good of the Tribes. The average mortal thinks the universe revolves around their own species." He sneered. "The mortal scientists we've worked with on this project are totally fixated on the goal of extending the lives of their own kind."

"So intent that they don't realize that they've made a devil's bargain with you?" she guessed.

"So intent that they don't care," he corrected. "Shall I tell you the whole story? Shall I shatter the beautiful illusions your Anthony fed you about his oh-so-noble Clans?"

Now that she knew how Anthony's own Matri had been the one to keep them apart, Rose doubted she would be disillusioned by any Tribe Prime's opinion of the vampire good guys.

"Tell me anything you'd like," she said. "I've got plenty of time. Apparently."

"The Clans are mad," he said. "The Families aren't much saner. Both deny their own natures. They are like wolves who've been bred into sheepdogs—a sick parody of what they should be, guarding their natural prey. Mating with their natural prey—"

"Don't tell me that the Tribes don't like mortal girls," she interrupted.

"Of course we do. But we would never breed with our female slaves. Clan Primes take mortal women as permanent mates and treat their offspring as beloved children. What they've created are half-breed mortal monsters and enemies within their midst."

"Why enemies?"

"These *children* of the Clans can never be like their sires. They are mules. They are mortal. They serve their Clan without truly being part of it. In the last century the mules' resentment has taken shape, festered, grown. The Tribes have helped stir the creatures toward rebellion."

"Tribes plural?" Rose questioned. "My understanding is that the Tribes fight with one another instead of cooperating."

"Times change: We have a loosely allied consortium these days. The Clans are the real enemy. The Families are not our friends. Once these other vampires are dealt with, I'm sure we'll fight among ourselves until one Tribe rules all the others. Until then, we are all the best of friends."

"But the Clans don't know this?"

"The Clans spend too much time protecting

mortals to watch their own backs. They are too noble to suspect traitors within their own ranks. Which brings us back to how you and I have come to this conversation. You see, many of the Clans' mortal offspring have made careers as scientists, working for the benefit of the Clans."

"They developed the drugs vampires use to live in the daylight," Rose guessed.

He nodded. "Those drugs help the sires of the mortal mules, but what's in it for them?"

"I suspect they're paid rather exorbitant salaries."

"What good is money when they're denied the longevity of their sires and bonded mortal mothers?"

"What's wrong with a normal mortal lifespan?" Rose countered.

"I wouldn't know; I don't have one. What I do know is that humans have always wanted immortality. I don't blame mortals for wanting to live as long as vampires. And I don't mind using their greed for longer life to help my Tribe acquire what we need."

"The daylight drugs," she said once again. "Anthony told me that if the drugs ever became useful, the Clans would do everything in their power to keep them out of the hands of the Tribes."

"They did become useful, and the Clans have

denied us access to them. They think we'd be more dangerous in the daylight."

"I'm sure they're right about that."

"Indeed they are. There is one way they'll allow a Tribe Prime access to their precious drugs—if we grovel and beg and humiliate ourselves by renouncing our history, our culture, and everything we believe in. If a Tribe Prime renounces his soul—"

"You have souls?"

"Deep souls," he responded. "Dark souls. Predator souls."

"Charming."

"Not at all." He gave her that dangerous smile again. "But I am comfortable with who I am, far more so than your Anthony will ever be."

"I don't think it's either your place or mine to discuss Anthony's soul. We can only speak for ourselves."

"You are quite correct. As females go, I have always found you interesting to talk to."

"You sound like some of the studio executives I used to deal with."

He looked offended at the comparison, and this almost amused her. But scoring points wasn't her goal, gathering information, was.

Rose returned to the subject. "So, the Tribes are working with the Clan traitors—"

"Among others," he added. "There are rogue werefolk involved. There are mortals looking to profit from the medical research. There are even some of the more fanatical vampire hunters in our conspiracy. We are a consortium of very strange bedfellows. We each have our own goals, but we are in complete agreement about one thing: the Clans, the Families, and the werefolk Council stand in our way, and we are going to destroy them."

"That's a rather ... *ambitious* goal." She wanted to say *crazy* but didn't want to lead the conversation off on another tangent.

"World domination is the actual goal, and that is truly ambitious. We are proceeding one step at a time. You are one of those steps. Or rather, the longevity project is."

"I'm the guinea pig, not the reason for what you did," she said, and he nodded. "Why'd you pick on me? How did you do it?"

And what price do I have to pay? She wondered, but she was damned if she was going to ask.

"The why is because you were old, you were unattached, and we knew that you had once shared blood with a Prime. We also believed that Tony would one day share blood with you again. An infusion of vampire blood was the necessary catalyst to activate the longevity drugs already in your system. It took him long enough to see you again. The night he finally showed up, I was getting ready to give you the infusion myself."

Infusion? Drugs *already* in her system? "How long has this been going on?"

"You have been receiving the treatment for over a year. The slow increase in the dosage has caused your body to change gradually until you were ripe for picking. There's been some discomfort," he added.

His ironic tone infuriated Rose. Now she understood the horrible, inescapable, growing pain that had driven her to the point of suicide. The pain had been caused by the drugs. It had been deliberate and evil.

"You've been torturing a little old lady!"

"Yes." He gestured toward the mirror. "But look at the results. Millions would kill for this treatment—hmmm, perhaps the promise of renewed youth would help recruit a mortal army. But for now, the plan is to reserve the process for a select few who can afford our price. Revolutions need financing."

Rose gaped at Gregor as he stood. He gently cupped her face in his hands and ran his thumbs across her cheeks and forehead. She flinched when he bent forward to brush his lips across hers.

"You are so lovely," he said, stepping away from her. "I hope it lasts."

Her mind reeled in horror. "Hope it l-lasts?"

Gregor walked to the door before turning to answer her. "One of the projected scenarios of the experiment is that the anti-aging effects can't be sustained without regular infusions of Prime blood. Since my presence is required elsewhere, I really do hope the donor I've arranged for you arrives in time," He shrugged. "If not—well, per-haps the scientists are wrong and you'll survive for a while. You'll be euthanized and dissected eventually anyway. Good-bye, my dear Rose. It has been a pleasure knowing you."

Rose stared at the closed door for a long time after he was gone, his chilling words ringing in her mind.

Chapter Forty

December 18, 4:00 PM
Shagal Citadel
Los Angeles, CA

Sid wondered if every vampire in Los Angeles was in the meeting room. As she took a seat and looked around, it became apparent that there were also werefolk representatives present. She found it curious, and a bit ominous, that there were no mortals present. If this was a meeting of everyone under Clan Shagal protection, where was Dr. Casmerek? And there were at least two mortal women bonded to local Primes; where were they?

"Where are Domini and Mia?" she asked.

"They are not here," Matri Serisa answered.

The Matri's cool tone told Sid that her question was not welcome. She also noticed from the glowering expressions of Alec Reynard and Colin Foxe that they weren't happy about their bondmates' absence.

Alec was Flare's brother. "Shouldn't you be protecting your bondmate?" she asked him.

"I most certainly should be," the Reynard Prime answered. He was glaring angrily at Tobias Strahan.

There was a lot of hostility in the room, most of it aimed at Tobias. For his part, Tobias stood in the center of the Council room like a great granite sea cliff unconcerned at the storm about to wash over it.

Who invited him here, anyway? She overheard Colin Foxe's thought.

She wasn't the only one who heard it; Joe held up his hand. "That would be me."

Sid hid a smile at Joe's cheeky response and saw by the quick flick of his gaze that he noticed it.

"What right does a werewolf have inviting a Prime into our territory?" a Shagal Prime demanded.

"He has the same right as any of the supernatural folk to protect our kind," Shaggy Harker, the alpha werewolf, said.

Sid thought the Shagal Prime looked like he was about to have a heart attack. This vampire had obviously never thought that not one, but two of the werefolk would ever talk back to him.

"We're in trouble. Tobias has brought his Angels to help," Shaggy continued.

"Help we don't need and didn't ask for," said a Prime with a rich Irish accent.

Sid looked at him with a start of surprise, discovering that Kiril had been correct about there being a vampire movie star. Sid figured he must be a Family Prime, as no Clan Matri would ever let one of her people lead such a public life.

"Thank you for your opinion, Jarrett," Elder Barak said to the actor. Jarrett certainly wasn't his stage name.

Jarrett turned proudly to Barak. "I realize I am a guest in Shagal territory, Elder, but I feel it is my duty to defend the place I call home."

"We all do," Colin Foxe said. "The last thing we need right now is outside interference."

"Are you going to keep snarling like pups or let Tobias have his say?" Shaggy nodded respectfully toward Lady Serisa. "Matri?"

The Matri folded her hands in her lap as everyone's attention focused on her. She was seated on a bench in front of the fireplace; Barak stood at her side, and her daughter, Cassie, sat beside her. Barak and Cassie were respected advisers, but all the power radiated from the small woman between them.

She turned that authority on Tobias Strahan. "Did I extend an invitation to you and your rabble that I don't recall? Why did you demand this meeting? And put restrictions on who could attend?"

So, Joe's phone call hadn't only brought his team leader to Los Angeles; Tobias had brought all of the Dark Angels. Now Sid understood why the locals were not happy.

"Thank you for agreeing to see me on such short notice, and for agreeing to my requests, Matri," Tobias answered.

"Your sudden appearance didn't really give me any choice, Tobias. We already have one emergency to deal with. My Primes do not have time for challenges and combat over etiquette issues at the moment."

"I agree. It is because of the attacks that I've brought in the Dark Angels."

Every other Prime in the room bristled. Fury, indignation, and hatred roiled through the psychically sensitive crowd.

Serisa held up a hand.

No one moved, and silence reigned. The riot subsided before it got the chance to begin.

"This is going to be boring if only dirty looks are thrown," Flare whispered to Sid.

Sid fought hard not to giggle and exchanged

an amused look with Joe. She looked away instantly, grateful that the focus was on Tobias.

She couldn't risk anyone noticing how comfortably her emotions resonated with the werewolf's. But what could she do? Other than stay away from him? She'd tried that and would have to try again. Her being half alive was better than Joe being all dead.

Chapter Forty-one

Those two are bound for trouble, Tony thought as he noted Sid and Bleythin's quick exchange. He made a note to have a stern talk with both of them, but his worries about Rose were paramount in his mind.

"Get on with it," he growled at the outsider whose appearance had just made things more complicated.

Tobias turned from the Matri to face him. "I've come to help." The sympathy in his eyes made Tony wonder just how much of his situation the other Prime knew. "I know that my belief that there is a war brewing among immortals isn't popular with everyone," he said, addressing his words to Matri Serisa once more. "But we found evidence that vampires and werefolk set the recent fires near San Diego. It was no coincidence that there have been fires set as part of the attacks on our kind here. The same people are involved. In San Diego, the intent was to cover their activities. In Los Angeles, the intent was to draw mortal attention to the immortals living among them. This was a different type of diversion, one meant to focus the vampire and werefolks' attention inward while they once more moved their base of operations."

Tony nodded in agreement. *He* was certainly diverted. Why had they picked on Rose? What did they want with her? Where had they taken her?

"Who are they?" he asked.

Kiril Wolf spoke up. "Purists. I'm sorry to contradict you, Prime Tobias, but your explanations are far too complicated. If there is a conspiracy, it is one organized by the fanatical branch of the vampire hunters."

The faintest of smiles played briefly across Tobias's features. "That's what they want you to think." He glanced toward Sid. "Lady Sidonie, what is your opinion of the evidence found at the wildfires?"

Nice move, Tony thought. The word of a

female always carried extra weight with Clan Primes. He saw by the amused lift of Sid's eyebrow, before she stood to address the room, that she was well aware of Tobias's maneuver.

"I think that there are still Tribe vampires involved in manufacturing knock-off versions of daylight drugs, and that they set the San Diego fires when they moved on. I think these same Tribe members have something to do with the nursing home fire and a missing mortal woman. I think that the nursing home was being used by bad guys, and it was time for them to move on again—so, another diversion. I think that Tobias Strahan is on to something, but I don't know what. I will speculate that the Purists are unknowingly being used by Tribe Primes to attack us. From the amount of media coverage, I'd say the attack was successful." She nodded toward Tobias and sat down.

"Media coverage," Tobias repeated. He looked around the room, catching one gaze after another. "Is that what you want?"

"We're working on covering our tracks," Shaggy Harker replied.

"How well can you hide your true existence when you're spending your time hunting Purists?" Tobias asked. "When you're guarding your homes and females instead of living your lives?"

"Werefolk females take care of themselves," Shaggy reminded the Prime.

"We could, too, if you'd let us," Flare added. And was ignored.

Tobias went on. "How can you hide in plain sight when each and every one of you deserts his daily life to protect our secret world? Don't you think mortals will notice? Don't you think that the Purists will turn media attention on your conspicuous absence?"

He pointed at Kiril. "Don't you have fires to fight?" At Alec Reynard. "You're a bodyguard: who's protecting your mortal clients right now?" At Colin Foxe. "Can you just walk away from SWAT team duty?" At Jarrett Baird. "Aren't you supposed to be on a movie set right now?" He addressed each Prime in turn, reminding them of the prominent roles they played in the outside world.

"You don't live in the dark anymore," he concluded. "But my team and I do. Let the Dark Angels deal with this matter." He gave Serisa a formal bow. "Give me permission to hunt freely in your territory, Matri."

"Great idea," Tony said before Serisa could respond.

The Matri glared at his enthusiasm. His rudeness was compounded a moment later when the phone in his jacket pocket rang.

Tony winced and pulled out the cell phone to turn it off. He caught his breath when he saw the number of the incoming calls.

"I've got to take this," he said.

"Anthony Crowe," Serisa called angrily as he turned to go.

He left the room without explanation or permission.

Chapter Forty-two

$\mathcal{J}$oe was tempted to add his own comments to Shaggy and the vampire woman's defense of women's independence, but a look from Tobias kept him quiet on the subject. He supposed the reason he'd been called to this meeting was to receive a scolding from the Matri. But since he was here, his job was to back up Tobias.

"Consider the advantage that the Tribes have over the Clans and Families," Joe said. "They're using that advantage against you right now."

Once again, Matri Serisa held up her hand to quell protests. "What advantage could there be?" she asked skeptically.

"They are much better at hiding than you are,"

Joe answered. "That makes it easier for them to expose the good guy vampires to the world, while they stay safe in the shadows. But if you go about your daily lives while the Dark Angels handle the attacks, there's much less chance of the mortals finding out about your private lives."

"We already know what happens when mortals find out about our kind," Serisa agreed. "There have been bloodbaths in the past."

"Yes, but it was mostly mortal blood that was shed," Barak contributed.

"That is so," she replied to her bondmate. "I regret every drop of mortal blood shed as much as I do the deaths of our own kinds. We've vowed to avoid violence in our current contacts with mortals."

"What have the Dark Angels vowed to do about mortal contacts?" Alec Reynard asked Tobias. "If the local Primes step aside and let you handle this problem, do you promise to avoid violence?"

"Not completely," Tobias answered honestly. "I've never had any compunction about terminating the Purists."

"Awright!" Colin Foxe said. "Maybe I should join you guys. Sorry, Matri," he added at Serisa's stern look.

"I agree that violence is to be used as a last

resort against mortals," Tobias went on. "But I won't rule out its use."

Serisa sighed. "I find that . . . acceptable."

"But, Matri, you aren't going to go along with these mercenaries' crazy idea—"

"Serisa has spoken." Barak cut Kiril Wolfgang off.

Joe waited for Tobias to protest about the Angels being called mercenaries, but when his commander ignored it, Joe managed to keep his own bristling anger under control. Tobias had what he'd come for: permission to let his hounds loose on the local bad guys. What mattered now was getting the job done.

Joe could barely keep from rubbing his hands together in anticipation. Then he looked at Sid, and Tobias's agenda suddenly wasn't so important to him.

As the room began to clear Joe made his way over to Sidonie. He cupped his palm under her elbow as she looked his way. The contact was disturbing as their skin touched and their gazes met.

"Let's talk."

She nodded, but they stood staring at each other, communicating, but without either words or telepathy. There was nothing in the world but them until a hand landed heavily on his shoulder.

"Are you being bothered, Lady Sidonie?" Kiril Wolfgang asked.

Joe turned on the young Prime with a snarl.

"You know Joseph and I are old friends," Sid answered Kiril.

"Friends, yes, but—"

"Go away, Kiril."

Her tone was soft. She was faintly smiling. And about as dangerous looking as Joe had ever seen her. Kiril went.

"How did you do that?" Joe asked her.

"We take lessons in Prime management from a young age. What was it you wanted to talk about?"

He couldn't remember why he'd approached her initially, though there were many things he needed to talk to her about. But his body wasn't interested in verbal communication, just scent, touch, taste—mating.

"Why am I half-crazed to have you when I hated your guts yesterday?"

Joe hadn't meant to say the words aloud, but when he looked around he saw that they were the only ones left in the room.

"You still hate my guts," she said. "The other stuff is just biology and chemistry. And proximity." She sounded very certain, but her gaze shifted away from him as she spoke.

"No, it isn't." Yes, it was. But . . . "It's more than that, and you know it."

"Please go back to being pissed off at me, Joe. It's better that way."

She managed to piss him off, all right. "Stop telling me what to do all the time. Do you ever stop giving orders? Do you ever stop making other people's decisions for them?"

"No."

Her simple answer turned his anger to curiosity. It still simmered beneath the surface, but the need for information took over.

"Why?"

"Why what?"

Her confusion made him smile. "Why do you have to *rule* everybody around you?"

Now Sid was getting angry. "I don't know. Why do you have to howl at the full moon?"

"I don't have to; I just like to. Maybe you just like being the boss all the time."

Or maybe she just didn't know any different.

"Of course I do. I'm a female. The Primes are aggressive. We females are—"

"Pack alphas." He supplied his own kind's term for her kind's behavior.

Sid nodded. "I guess that comes close enough."

"Actually, there's a huge difference between how vampire and werewolf females think and act. And the difference makes werewolves better."

Sid crossed her arms and lifted her chin belligerently. "Oh, yeah? How so?"

"No alpha female arbitrarily decides the fate of any other adult pack members."

"Werewolves act for the good of the pack," she reminded him.

"Always, but the process is a bit more democratic."

"But just a bit."

"And we treat one another like adults. We can make our own decisions about our private lives."

"Lucky you," she said. Her defensive posture relaxed a little. She put a hand up. "All right, I admit that taking your memories away without asking was wrong. It was high-handed and unethical. But it was for your own good, damn it!"

"You should have asked first!" he shouted back. "But that isn't how vampire females do it, is it? You just decide what's for the best, and never mind what anyone else thinks."

"Joe—I—"

"You should have explained *why* you needed to seal yourself from me, Sidonie! You should have treated me like an adult!"

Chapter Forty-three

Sid stumbled backward into a chair and covered her face with her hands, fighting down the sob that threatened to escape her throat. She refused to shed the tears burning her eyes.

Afraid that all the emotional turmoil between her and Joe would bring the other psychics in the house to see what was wrong, she fought for calm. The thought of a squad of protective Primes showing up terrified her. She wasn't going to let her years of protecting Joe go to waste now because her own wounds were open and bleeding.

"Stop making me want to cry," she mumbled behind her hands. "Stop making this so hard."

"Why shouldn't it be hard for both of us?"

Sid put her hands down and looked up at Joe, expecting the stony expression he'd turned on her when they'd first met again. That wasn't what she saw at all. There was pain in his eyes, but sympathy and compassion as well.

She gazed back warily. "What are you looking at me like that for?"

"I can't tell you."

Sid wasn't sure whether she was amused or furious. She was on the verge of complete, exhausted defeat. She gave a faint laugh. "Playing vampire games, are you? I suppose I deserve it."

"I can't tell you because I'm not sure how I'm looking at you."

She let him lie to her. It was only fair.

"I have been a fool," she said. "A complete and utter fool."

"You followed your instincts."

"Don't you go defending me, Joseph Bleythin."

"At least you responded in the way you were raised to handle trouble," he went on. "There *is* some sort of trouble involved, isn't there?"

"I reacted; I didn't think. I can't change anything now."

"Have you considered that maybe *we* could change this thing, whatever it is?"

She shook her head and watched the angry tension fill him again.

"Then at least tell me why, Sidonie. Make me understand. Did you sleep with a werewolf to try to forget being raped by your own kind?"

"Would that make what I did forgivable? Would it let me off the hook?"

"It would make it understandable."

She wished she could tell him that was the reason, that their problems stemmed from what the Tribe bastards had done to her. But she'd only been able to deceive him once.

"Your timing's off, Joe. Our affair was before my run-in with the Manticore Tribe."

"Then—"

She stood quickly and put her fingers over his lips. "This isn't the time or place for the explanation you deserve."

She shivered when he kissed her fingers. His lips were warm and soft, the kiss maddeningly gentle. She wanted so much more than a kiss . . .

"Damn it, Joe—"

He grabbed her shoulders and pulled her close. He knew too well what she—what they both— needed. Her mouth opened hungrily beneath his. Their tongues twined and teased.

They both heard a door open and were apart in an instant, but Sid didn't think it was quick enough. Her body still buzzed with desire as she turned to face the door.

Lady Serisa stood there for a moment, her expression completely blank, before she stepped back and closed the door.

"Think she saw us?" Joe asked. "Think she cared? Should she have cared?"

Sid was gripped by too much fear to answer him. Dear, conservative cousin Kiril must have ratted them out.

Chapter Forty-four

"Stupid, stupid, stupid," she said at last. "I am *so* stupid."

Joe gaped at her. "What are you talking about?"

The expression in her eyes was suddenly wild. "Run! Hide. Get away from me!"

He'd never seen her like this before. "Are you hysterical?" he asked.

"Pretty close," Sid answered.

"Why?"

"A female vampire getting caught kissing a werewolf by a Matri—you figure it out."

"I didn't mean to embarrass you. But aren't unbonded females encouraged to make love to whoever they want?"

She waved her hands in front of her. "Never mind that. We have more important things to do right now. Tobias needs you, and I have to find Rose."

She turned around and walked away. Joe's head spun as he watched her go. For a second he was consumed by a stab of hunger as he took in the sway of her hips and the shapely length of her legs. He realized that his response to her wasn't just recovered memory; she was getting sexier all the time. Every moment he was with her made him want her all the more.

Even worse, he admired her. She'd betrayed him, and yet . . . She wouldn't let him give her excuses for her actions. She was determined to find the missing woman.

And she was protecting him, wasn't she?

It hadn't been embarrassment that radiated from Sidonie when the Matri saw them together. He should have noticed it instantly, but lust must have dulled his senses. He was aware now of the lingering scent of terror in the room.

"Idiot," he muttered at himself.

He remembered something Laurent had said back at the camp. *"If you're in love with her, it's a good thing you left, because I can't think of a quicker way for you to get yourself killed."*

At the time, he'd thought the words were a brotherly warning not to hurt Sid. Now he suspected that the Wolf Clan Prime had been speaking literally.

What dark secrets were the vampires hiding?

Did she somehow, some way, believe that what she'd done when she took his memories was protecting his life? How did that make sense to her? If that *was* the reason. Or was he trying to give himself another reason to forgive her?

He had to know.

"Lucy, you got some 'splainin' to do," he murmured, and hurried after her.

But when he caught up to Sid in front of the Citadel, the wide brick courtyard was crawling with vampires. The thought gave him a horror movie image, when in fact nobody was crawling and there were five Primes in sight doing their jobs: two guards at the entrance, another pair by the front gates, and the fifth on patrol around the intersection of the house, the front garden, and the multicar garage. Sid was standing in the center of the courtyard, circled by the males of her kind. The Primes were all going about their duties, but Joe could tell that they were all also intensely interested in the female's presence.

Sid's eyes were closed, her attention focused inward. Joe cautiously approached her. She swore as he reached her side and took her cell phone out of its belt clip.

"When telepathy doesn't work . . ." she grumbled.

"Try technology," he finished for her. "Who are you calling?"

"Tony. He's not in the house. No one's seen him since he left the meeting. Can you . . ." She waved a hand through the air.

"Sniff him out?" Joe shook his head. "You know what being around a bunch of vamps does to our noses."

"His car's gone." She shut the phone with an annoyed snap. "He's not answering the phone, and his psychic shields are buttoned up tight."

"Which means he doesn't want to be contacted."

She nodded. "But why? Something to do with Rose, I bet." She put her hands on her hips. "No doubt he's off trying the usual Clan boy heroics. He's going to need my help. He brought me in on this op, and I'm in until he tells me different."

"But you need to find him first." Joe thought through his options, then went with his gut—and his heart. "Tobias hasn't pulled me off working with you, and I told you I'd help find Ms. Cameron. I think I have a way of tracking her down."

"Then that's what we have to do."

He was pleased that she didn't argue about his

help. They had fallen easily into their old partnership. Maybe she'd missed it as much as he had. He wondered if she'd told herself that she didn't miss it as often as he had.

"How do you plan to track her?" Sid asked curiously.

"Roses." Joe smiled at her confusion and led the way toward the garage where her SUV was parked.

Chapter Forty-five

Sid followed his directions and didn't ask Joe any questions on the drive. She was too consumed with trying to convince herself that nothing had happened with that kiss that they needed to be concerned about.

He told her to stop the car in front of the burned hulk of the nursing home.

"What are we doing back here?" she asked.

"Hunting for roses." He got out of the car.

Sid frowned and followed. "Is there more than one Rose we're looking for?" she asked. "I think Tony collected a single Rose and not a bouquet of them."

Joe just smiled in reply. He moved across the grass toward what was left of the building.

The grounds were completely dark, the garden in trampled ruins and still soaked from the water used to fight the fire. Sid took a careful look around, watching her partner's back as she always did. Only when she was satisfied that the ruins were as deserted as they seemed did she join him.

Though he was still in human shape, she could tell that he was concentrating with his werewolf senses.

"What are you hunting?"

He frowned at the distraction, but explained. "For some reason they took everything in the room when they took her, including the several dozen roses Tony sent her for their anniversary."

"He sent her roses?" Sid was as indignant as she was incredulous. "No one's ever sent me roses."

Joe shrugged. "The older generation's more romantic, I guess."

"You think the roses and Rose are still together, and you're hunting for their scent?"

"I picked the smell up earlier. I think it must still be here."

Sid gestured. "Then do your thing."

He nodded and returned to walking around the ruins taking slow, deep breaths.

Standing back to keep her vampire energy out of his nose's way, she recalled, "When I telepathically searched for her, I saw colors: pink and yellow and . . . rose colors. I think I was seeing where she's being held."

He flashed Sid a toe-curling smile. "Coming at the same thing from different angles, as usual."

"As usual," She repeated.

They smiled at each other, but the moment of joyous communication passed instantly. They stared into each other's eyes. Joe's expression hardened, and all his tension and anger came roaring back with a force that rocked Sid down to her soul.

"I had to!" The words burst out of her in a helpless wail of anguish. "I couldn't—"

She turned away from him as she bit off the words. His hands were on her shoulders instantly, and there was no gentleness in his touch.

His breath was hot on the back of her neck. His voice was a low, dangerous rasp. "You couldn't what?"

Sid closed her eyes as the terror she'd lived with for so long washed through her.

"You couldn't what?" he repeated. "I smell the fear, Sidonie. Vampires can't hide every emotion from us. That fear isn't *of* me."

Sid tried to fake a semblance of calm. She shook off his touch and stepped away, trying to make her movements seem casual. She turned to haughtily face Joe. "Of course I'm not afraid of a werewolf," she told him.

"You're a bad actress, Sidonie."

"And you're—nosy!" she threw back at him.

To her surprise they both laughed, but not an iota of tension was eased between them.

"You told me I deserved an explanation," he told her.

"Yes, but—" She gestured, a quick, nervous jerk of her hands. "We need to find—"

"I'm not waiting for a time and place of your choosing." His harsh voice crackled between them. "Right now. Right here. Talk to me."

He stepped close again, put his hands on her again. The pressure of his nearness, his touch, was both threatening and comforting. She couldn't run away any longer.

"Female vampires bond with Primes," she answered. "*Only* with Primes. Do you understand?"

The sounds of freeway traffic roared in the distance, with the murmur of the ocean beyond sounding in the night, but silence reigned for a long time between them. Sid waited, shaking a little, sometimes remembering that even vampires need to breathe.

"No," he finally answered.

She let out her breath in an exasperated rush. "How can a member of a psychic species be so dense?"

"We're from different psychic species," he answered. "I only know how werefolk bond."

"See? You do get it!"

"What? That you can't bond with anyone but another vampire?"

"No! I'm not *allowed* to bond with anyone but a Prime. There's a big difference between what's possible and what—"

"Are you saying that we could be bonded if we wanted—"

"What either of us *want* hasn't got a damn thing to do with it. Joseph, if they discover what I've done, the Furies will be let loose for sure. Or the Primes will act on their own."

As she spoke, she could almost feel eyes on them in the dark. She looked around, all her senses alert for the presence of hunters surrounding them.

"We're alone." His tone was assured, but not reassuring.

She knew he was right, but the fear of the hunt weighed on her.

"What have you done?" he asked.

"Fallen in love with you." But that wasn't the sin. It brought her pain, but it wasn't what put his life in danger. "I tasted you," she confessed. "I took your blood more than once during those days we spent in Cabo."

"You bit me." He nodded. "I remember. Now."

"I made you forget to save your life," she told him. "If it is ever discovered that I'd begun to bond with someone other than a vampire—"

"Wait a minute," he cut her off. "Primes bond with mortal women all the time."

"But I'm not a Prime! The rules are different for females."

"You've always broken those rules."

"No, I haven't. I've skirted around the edges, but there's only so far even I could go. Until I fell in love with you," she added. "I crossed the line then, and I've tried very hard to protect you from the danger I put you in. I acted selfishly, stupidly. The crime is mine, but you'll pay with your life if they ever find out."

"I still don't understand. I remember what you did. I remember what you told me in the garden three years ago. In my dreams I can hear the fountain in background, smell the flowers, feel the moonlight. They aren't dreams, they're nightmares. But it really happened, and the humiliation of what you said sticks to me like cold sweat."

"Joe, I—"

"Do you remember any of that, Sidonie?"

Chapter Forty-six

Three Years Ago
San Diego, CA
Clan Wolf Citadel

"*Lucy, you got some 'splainin' to do.*"

Joe was furious. He tried to cover it with curiosity, he tried to cover it with humor, but he felt the anger growing into a raging fire. Just how badly had she betrayed him? Made a fool of him?

Suspicion gnawed at him as he confronted Sid.

"Explaining?" She tried to smile, but her expression was tense. She couldn't look him in the eye for more than a moment. "I don't—"

"You told me that vampires and werewolves couldn't possibly be attracted to each other. You've had me convinced for years that all we *could ever be was good friends. I've been going along thinking—believing—that the partnership was enough."*

"We are best friends," she said. "The best of partners. Why—"

"I just found out that our friend Cathy and her Hunyara cousin are the descendants of a mating between Primes and werewolves. So don't try to tell me that we can't be more than friends."

"I didn't know anything more about the Hunyaras than you did!" she protested.

He could believe that, but he knew as sure as life that there were other lies she was hiding. "You've done something to me—messed with me."

"Why would you think that?"

He touched the side of her nose. "You don't have any sex scent to me. I should be able to sense your gender and every nuance of arousal—from vague interest in a passing stranger to complete turn-off—from you even if we were just friends. You read neutral to me. You took that part of yourself away from me. What are you hiding from me, Sidonie?"

"Damn!" She turned her back on him.

He pulled her back around. "Are you angry at yourself because you did too good a job messing with my head?"

"*You know me too well, Joseph.*"

At least she wasn't denying it. "*What happened?*"

She lifted her head, and this time she held his gaze. "We had an affair."

His senses reeled. "We what?"

"*You heard me.*"

"*I don't love you,*" he said.

"*Yes, you do. You just don't remember.*"

"*What are you talking about?*"

"*We've been lovers, Joe. I made you forget. It was just a fling,*" she went on coldly. "*It shouldn't have happened. I didn't want to mess up our partnership with any trivial baggage—so I made you forget.*"

December 19, 12:03 AM, Present Day
Los Angeles, CA

"You even lied about the lie!" Joe accused. "You told me it was just a fling that you made me forget. And you made me believe it!"

"Well—yeah," Sid answered. "And now you remember what really happened. But knowing what we really shared doesn't make you feel any better, does it?"

"You sent me away hating you."

"I didn't send you anywhere. You ran off to join the foreign legion on your own." She took a deep breath that sounded almost like a sob. "I was glad you went, though. I tried to be strong for you, but being near you was a constant temptation. I had to protect you from me."

"Oh, please—"

"I'm not joking! I'm a vampire, damn it! I crave blood—your blood and only yours. You're all I want in every way a female can want a male, and if my people find out, you will die." She put her hands on his shoulders and shook him. "Do you understand *now* why I did what was necessary to save your life? I put you at risk. I'll suffer the consequences of my own selfish lust, but I'll be damned if I let them kill the man I love! Find yourself a werewolf girl and forget about me."

He pulled her close. "I don't want a werewolf girl."

Sid twisted out of his arms and backed away, her hands covering her mouth. Her eyes glowed red, and she closed them until she got herself under control. When she looked at him they were blue once more. She put her hands down when she no longer had to hide her fangs. He knew that she was barely under control, but her reactions amazed him.

She loved him.

She'd acted for his own good. He wished she'd explained sooner, given him a choice, but that was a vampire for you—especially the females. When Sid decided to save you, she didn't go halfway. He recalled the tattoos currently marking her body. The hours spent getting the work done must have been excruciatingly painful, but she'd done it to save a girl who needed her help.

"Can we please go save Rose now?" She interrupted his thoughts.

Joe ran his hands through his hair. This was one more person she was committed to helping, and he'd promised to partner with her in the search for the little old lady.

"Yeah. I guess we should."

Chapter Forty-seven

Minds didn't change with age, bodies just got harder to deal with. Rose had known that for a very long time. She was brand new, but she was still herself. And her self was hungry. She was also nervous and restless and bored, and so angry she could spit nails as the hours passed and her captors left her alone.

She sat on the bed with her chin on her propped up knees and blushed when she finally put a name to the other thing she was feeling. It was also a kind of hunger.

"Well, isn't that just . . . typical," she complained, and slid off the bed to stand barefoot on the cool hardwood floor.

She wiggled her toes. Yep, that felt good.

She stretched, then twirled around and tried a karate kick like she'd seen in movies. That landed her on her butt, but she let out a joyous laugh just the same. If she'd tried that a few days ago, she'd have broken a hip for sure. Not that she would have tried anything so silly then.

"Now I know why it's called *hard*wood," she muttered as she got easily to her feet. She tried a few of the dance steps she'd learned so very long ago. "A product of the studio system learns many useful skills."

For example, she could fence and ride and dance and sing (though not well), walk like a model, talk like a duchess.

The studio had not taught her how to pick locks. That was a skill that might have been useful, had there been anything but a smooth surface to the door when she went to check it. That was one way in which this cell was different from her room at Ocean View.

She walked around the room, checking everything, noting the differences along with the similarities. She refused to look in the mirror and refused to think about the fear, but she wanted to scream. She went into the bathroom and took a shower, but the feel of the warm water, the smooth, fragrant lather, and her own hands on her young skin nearly drove her mad.

"Bad idea," she muttered.

She dried off briskly, avoided looking into the bathroom mirror, tied on a very plush terry robe, and went back to exploring her surroundings. The soft cloth against her damp, naked skin was disconcerting.

The roses were beginning to fade. Which was no comfort at all considering the irony that she was brand new while the flowers were dying. She and Anthony would have laughed about it together, if he'd been there. She buried her face in a bouquet and took deep breaths, glad that the fragrance was still delightful. How she'd counted on the annual arrival of Anthony's Christmas gift every year! She appreciated the way they reminded her of him still, no matter how odd the circumstances.

But being reminded of him only made things worse.

Her fists were clenched tightly at her sides when she finally went to look out the window. She didn't know why she'd put it off for so long. Maybe it was that every change in her environment, even the littlest ones, frightened her. Seeing the view from her prison cell was certainly not a small change; it showed conclusively how different her world now was.

Not a prison, she reminded herself. *I'm a lab rat.*

She had been for a long time. She didn't yet know if being aware of the experimentation made it worse.

Instead of the yellow hibiscus bush outside her window, she saw daylight fading and mountains that were green from winter rain and full of gathering shadows. Acres of pastureland and a distant line of trees separated the house from the hills. She caught a glimpse of a gated fence and a dirt driveway through the barred window. The room was at least three stories off the ground. If there were guards she didn't spot them. She could hear traffic, but in the far distance. She was on a ranch, she decided. How far from Los Angeles? She'd been an invalid for the last six years, first living with a nurse in her home before moving to Ocean View. She didn't get out much, and the city changed and grew constantly. She thought they'd brought her somewhere isolated, yet not far from the city, but that was only a guess.

Oh, Anthony! Rose thought, picturing him in her mind, hoping the telepathic link he claimed they shared would work.

She closed her eyes and mentally pictured herself jumping up and down and waving. *I'm here, dear. Please come get me.*

No answering thought came back to her through the ether. But all her senses were alive and sensitized with the thought of him. She felt the weight of her young breasts and growing heat between her legs.

"Oh, dear."

She hugged herself around the waist and turned from the window.

As much as she would have liked to deny it, she was feeling . . . frisky.

Was there something about being in hopeless danger that stirred the sexual part of her? Experience would say that there was.

December 22, 1944
Bastogne, Belgium

Anthony's excuse for making her hide in the attic of the abandoned house was that it was better not to disturb the commander of the American forces defending the town with the knowledge that there was a female civilian in their midst. As if there weren't plenty of other female civilians to worry about; not all the natives had been able to flee the fighting. The people who'd tried to peacefully live here were as trapped as the Ameri-

can troops surrounded by German Panzer units.

"As if General McAuliffe didn't have more to worry about than one lost USO hoofer," she complained as she lay on her back and stared at the ceiling. Dust sifted down from above as a shell exploded nearby. The old building shook a little, then shook again as another shell hit closer still.

Rose shivered. She'd lived in California for a year, so she knew what earthquakes felt like. They were scary enough, but the random shaking of the earth wasn't anywhere near as frightening as the continuous barrage of huge guns from the enemy Tiger tanks. Earthquakes weren't deliberately trying to kill you.

Fear coiled inside her, and she wanted to cover her ears and scream in terror. Instead, she concentrated on her annoyance with her traveling companion.

She was certain Anthony Crowe had her hiding in this dark, freezing cell because he was the one who wasn't supposed to be here. He was a vampire. He lived by night, and he lived in secret. His habit was to hide. Stashing her away while he skulked around in the dark was just his way of operating.

He got to be heroic. She had to wait here like a lady in a tower, when she could have been helping at the field hospital. She hated waiting.

And why was she doing what he told her to?

Rose stood, preparing to leave, but the little trapdoor in the floor opened before she could move. Anthony crawled into the attic and closed the opening after him.

He grinned, white teeth flashing in the dim light. "Guess what just happened?"

How could she possibly know anything that was going on? "We surrendered?" she asked sarcastically.

"The Germans sent a note asking us to. Do you know what General McAuliffe said to that?"

Rose had to bend over in the cramped space to step up to Anthony. "How would I know anything?" she snarled.

He was so amused he didn't notice her anger. "He said 'Nuts.' That was his official answer to the German commander—'Nuts.'"

Terror flashed through Rose while Anthony chuckled at the general's bravado.

Nuts. A flat-out refusal to surrender to the overwhelming force that completely surrounded the town. There was too much cloud cover for air support to help the trapped Americans. God knew when or if reinforcements could get to them.

"We're going to die," Rose said. "I'm going to die."

Anthony's arms came around her. "Don't be afraid."

She held him close, too aware of his hard male body, "I'm not afraid to die." She looked him in the eye. "But I'll be damned if I'm going to die a virgin."

Chapter Forty-eight

Anthony held her out at arm's length. "What are you talking about?"

"You know exactly what I'm talking about." She grabbed him by the front of his coat. She tried pulling him back to her, but he wouldn't budge. "I want you to make love to me, Anthony!"

"That's not going to happen, young lady."

"I'm not a lady, I'm an actress."

"You're still too young."

A loud explosion shook the house and he pulled her close again. She dug her fingers nervously into his shoulders.

"I'm not going to get much older if this keeps

up," Rose pointed out. "You've already drunk my blood. That's pretty intimate, isn't it?"

"Very." A wicked smile played around his lips. She very much wanted those lips kissing her.

"Then how much different is making love?"

"They're closely related," he admitted. He glanced around the small, dim attic. They were standing hunched over to keep their heads from bumping the low ceiling. "Hardly a romantic setting."

She nodded. "And it's freezing cold in here, too. I don't care. Make love to me, Anthony."

"What if the building gets hit while we're performing the act? Do you want to die bare naked in a compromising position?"

Rose giggled. "We don't have to be bare naked. If I understand the mechanics, only the lower parts need to be exposed. It's too cold to take our clothes off, anyway."

He kissed the top of her head. "Practical creature." She pushed aside his coat and began to unbutton the shirt beneath, just far enough to kiss his exposed throat. He gave a gasp of pleasure, and she fumbled to unfasten his belt.

"Young lady, I take it that you intend to have your way with me, no matter how much I protest." He didn't try to stop her.

"Help me," she said.

In response, his hands slid up under her layered shirts to cup her breasts. His mouth came down on hers, drinking in her moan of pleasure.

Present Day

"And things just went on from there," Rose murmured, sitting on the bed, staring at her feet. Her toes were tightly curled against the pale wood floor. A lifetime's worth of pent-up desire coursed through her.

She realized she'd been shaken out of the erotic memory by the sound of the door opening, and stood. A knot of fear twisted her insides, but she managed a mask of bravado as she faced the doorway.

"Please tell me you've finally brought food— Well, it's about time you got here," she said as Anthony Crowe was shoved roughly into the room.

"I knew you wouldn't want to start the party without me." His voice was slurred and his eyes were dull, but he managed to smile at her.

"You're naked." She rushed to him as the door slammed shut behind him.

"You've never minded before," he said as he collapsed into her arms.

Rose managed to swing him around onto the bed before his weight dragged them both to the floor. Not only was he naked and groggy, but his hands were cuffed behind his back. He continued to smile at her. Somehow it eased her terror.

"I don't mind now," she told him. She settled beside him and ran her fingers through his thick black hair. "But you look awful. How did you find me? How did you get captured?"

"Didn't. Someone called to tell me where you were at. Got a call from your cell phone," he tried to clarify. "I saw your phone last year and found out your number."

"What?" Rose jumped to her feet. "You deliberately walked into a trap? I don't know why I let Gregor convince me I needed a cell phone at my age—Gregor!" she spat out angrily.

"Gregor," Anthony confirmed. "Told me to come alone if I wanted you to live. Very melodramatic fellow. Looking forward to killing him." His voice became slower and fainter with each word.

Rose patted Anthony's bare shoulder. "I'm looking forward to your killing him, too."

"Give you his head for a present." His eyes slowly closed.

"Thank you, dear. That would be nice."

She was aware of the instant Anthony became

unconscious. His vulnerability sent cold dread through her.

"Idiot. How could you put yourself in danger like this?" But she loved him desperately and deeply for his putting his life on the line for her and wanted nothing more than to protect him.

All she could try to do was make him comfortable, which he certainly couldn't be with his hands fastened behind him. She rolled him onto his side and propped a pillow behind his back. When that didn't do any good, she squeezed herself onto the narrow bed beside him. It took some time before she managed to wriggle and heave them into a position where she could hold him in her arms, his head resting on her shoulder. His body was warm and heavy and wonderfully solid against the length of hers, and his steady breathing subconsciously calmed her.

She sighed and held him close. After a while, she felt safe enough to follow him into sleep.

Chapter Forty-nine

"This is another fine mess you've gotten me into." Tony meant the words as a joke, but the rasp of pain in his voice made him fear Rose might take him seriously.

"I think you got yourself into it," she answered calmly. "I do appreciate the sentiment, but turning yourself in to the bad guys was stupid."

"It was a romantic gesture."

"Less romance in the future, more practical solutions, please."

He grunted in reply. Rose's fingers stroked through his hair. He couldn't bear to let her know how much the slightest touch hurt—not when he loved her to touch him, no matter what.

Tony ignored the agony filling his head and attempted to get his bearings. He couldn't quite bring himself to open his eyes yet. He decided that his head rested on her shoulder. Lovely. He felt her stretched out beside him, the softness and warmth of her skin connected to his along the length of their bodies. Nice.

The pain kept him from any psychic awareness of Rose, but he was instinctively aware of the call of her life-giving blood. The girl always had made his fangs ache.

"I vant to dreenk your blood."

She patted his head. "You go right ahead, dear."

"When I'm sober," Tony added reluctantly. "I don't know what was in the shot they gave me, but I'm not up to much just yet." He let out a moan when Rose gently eased away from him, instantly missing her warmth and softness. "Aw, honey!"

"Try sitting up," was her cruel response. She took him by the shoulders and helped him.

Once his feet were flat on the floor and the rest of him was stable enough that, with effort, he wasn't going to fall over, Tony forced himself to open his eyes. This brought a fresh shot of pain, but the sunburst brightness soon faded to blobs and shadows.

At least he could now remember who he was

and how he got there; he hadn't been able to for a while after he first came awake. He hoped the effects of the shot would soon be completely out of his system. He'd gotten the impression from his gleeful captors that they thought one dose would keep him helpless for several days. Unfortunately, being drug-free wouldn't help the headache or the psychic disruption from the subsonic screech of the zapper they used to shield the hideout, but one thing at a time.

"You are far from all right," Rose said.

His gaze followed the sound of her voice and eventually, the blob right in front of him resolved into Rose's form. She was wearing a short, pale pink bathrobe. It showed off her glorious gams, and the top gaped loose enough to give him a nice view of her bosom.

The sight brought a smile to his lips, and a shot of desire warmed his blood. If his hands weren't fastened by silver handcuffs, he'd have tugged off the belt that kept the robe precariously closed.

Rose passed her hand in front of his face. "What are you smiling about?" She gasped as her gaze moved to his groin. "Anthony Crowe, are you lusting at a time like this?"

"Do I hear indignation from the woman who practically raped me during the Battle of the Bulge?"

"Funny you should mention that, because—" She caught herself and looked at him with narrow-eyed suspicion. She turned around slowly and asked when she faced him again, "Have you by any chance noticed anything . . . *different* about me since the last time we met?"

Tony gave Rose a thorough looking over, from the tips of her pretty pink toes to the top of her coppery red head.

He tilted his head sideways. "Are you wearing your hair differently?" he asked in puzzlement.

She was not amused. He could tell by the way her big eyes narrowed and her lush lips thinned and how her fine skin went alabaster pale. She took a deep breath.

"Sometimes when you get really angry, I think your freckles are going to explode," he added.

The air rushed out of her in a laugh instead of a furious yell. "You are impossible," she told him, but her gaze had softened.

"You are the most beautiful woman in the world."

"Maybe in 1944—no, I was still a skinny teen-ager then. In 1952 I was incredibly gorgeous, and I would have accepted the compliment then. But we've moved into a new millennium, darling, and I should be dead, not"—she ran a hand down her sleek, elegantly curved body—"new."

"You've never looked any different to me."

"This is not the time for charming lies, Anthony."

"I am a psychic who fell in love with your mind and spirit and soul. Do you think I have ever given a damn about your appearance?"

"Yes."

It was his turn to laugh. "All right, you've got me there. Of course I lust after your luscious body. But I love *you*."

"Luscious! I haven't been—oh, never mind, we went through this discussion days ago. What day is it, anyway?"

He glanced toward the room's one window. "It's night." He looked at her again. "And you're about to tell me that's the most sensible thing I've said since I woke up. And—" Tony swiveled his head to follow her as she rushed around to the other side of the bed. "Where are you going?"

She pulled open a drawer in the bedside table. She rummaged around and after a few moments gave a deliciously wicked, triumphant laugh. "Idiots! I don't know why the fools brought all my stuff with me, but it's their own fault." She held up a small red leather case and waved it triumphantly. "My husband left me this."

Tony grimaced at the reference to the late Thad

Pearson, even though he now knew Pearson's relationship with Rose had been platonic.

He craned his head as Rose knelt on the floor beside the bed and unzipped the case. "What is it?"

"A manicure set, among other things." She slid a nail along a section on the inside of the case and flipped open a panel beneath the grooming instruments. Rose grinned up at him.

"Are those lockpicks?"

"Thad claimed he was a stage magician before he got into movies, but I think he might have been a cat burglar. He taught me a few things."

"At least not in bed," Tony grumbled.

She chortled at his jealousy. "Stretch your hands back, and hold still." She tugged on the cuffs and he winced. "Are these things silver? Of course they are; you wouldn't still be wearing them if they were anything else. Damn those bastards! There are burn marks on your wrists."

"There won't be for long when you get them off."

"Be patient. I'm out of practice. With everything," she added with a deep sigh.

But soon he heard a grunt of triumph, a sharp click, and then came the sweet, instant cessation of the burning pain as the silver fell away from his wrists.

With his hands finally free, he grabbed Rose

and pulled her onto the bed. "You're getting plenty of practice from now on," he promised.

His hands shook as he ripped the belt from the robe to get to her naked flesh. He breathed in her scent, ran his tongue over the inside curves of her breasts. The reality of Rose was better than even the most vivid memories.

His voice was rough with the desire he'd had to deny all these years. "And now we're going to practice every way a man and woman can bring each other pleasure."

Chapter Fifty

She wanted Anthony's hands on her.

"Not dreams." He spoke her thought.

"Not memories." She spoke his.

"Now and forever," he told her.

He pressed her back against the bed, his weight hard and real. Her fingers played over his skin, finding nothing soft about him. He was all hard muscle and pent-up tension.

Rose closed her eyes as a lifetime of loneliness and longing flowed away. Sensation took the place of thought.

"Heaven," she whispered. "I've died and gone to heaven."

"Better than heaven," he said.

The sharp prick of pain when he bit her breast sent a burning rush of ecstasy through her. Rose's fingers clamped onto Anthony's shoulders as she tried to hang on for dear life.

What are you holding on to? his seductive thought whispered in her mind.

Sanity, she thought back. *The world.*

Let yourself go. I'm with you.

His touch, his thoughts, his solid, virile presence were all she needed, all she wanted. Anthony brought her back to life and—

Rose screamed.

She couldn't stop. The sound went on and on, even though a small part of her mind tried to make it stop. Even though Anthony held her close, held her still when she clawed at him.

"By the Lady of the Moon, woman, do you know how much of a headache I already have."

These were the first words that made any sense to Rose, although she thought he'd been speaking to her the whole time the panic ran its course.

"Get away from me," she said. "Don't touch me."

He let her go and backed away, leaving her sitting alone on the bed. Her fingers dug into the side of the mattress. Her throat ached. Her face was wet, and there was the taste of salt in her mouth.

"My vision's blurred," she rasped. "I can barely see you. I'm getting old again."

Anthony disappeared and she heard the sound of running water. He came back and handed her a warm, damp washcloth. "You've been crying, that's all," he told her. "Wash your face and you'll feel better."

She responded to the tone of gentle command and did as he said. Though her eyes burned, her vision did clear as soon as she wiped away the tears. She'd been breathing in wild, ragged pants, but the painful racing of her heart was calming down.

"What was that all about?" she asked.

"You're the one who had the fit, darling—you tell me." He rubbed his temples. "You could have made a fortune as a scream queen in horror movies."

"I am in a horror movie. Only it's real."

"Hey, just because your boyfriend's a vampire—"

"I'm the monster!" She was on her feet shouting, and she couldn't stop. "I'm not real! I'm this horrible construction! Frankenstein's monster! I'm the result of a horrible experiment! I'm an abomination!"

"No, you're *not*!"

Anthony's shout was a roar of fury that shook

her into silence. Rose stared as he grabbed her by the shoulders.

"What did those bastards tell you? What kind of nonsense did this Tribeson Gregor feed you? Whatever he said was a lie." He put his fingers under her chin and forced her to look him in the eyes. "You and I are of one blood. Whatever it is that flows in me that keeps me young, flows in you."

Rose jerked her head away from his touch. "That's what he said—that your blood was the catalyst that made the experiment work."

"You *did* need my blood, but that was the only truth he told you. Everything else must have been a con game he was running on these mortal scientists to get something he wanted from them." Tony shook his head. "No one made you a monster. I claimed you as my bondmate. The rejuvenation worked a lot faster than I thought it would—and I wasn't even sure it would work at all—but it's our connection that brings us to where we are right now."

She tilted her head sideways. "Are you sure?"

"Your skepticism wounds me."

"I think you're trying to make me feel better so you can get into my pants."

"You're not wearing any," he reminded her. His eyes glittered mischievously. "Do you feel better?"

She sighed. "I feel exhausted."

"Hysteria will do that to you."

She reached out and brushed a wave of black hair back from his forehead. "And you have a headache."

"The bastards have a zapper going. But I'm not using it as an excuse to say 'Not tonight, dear.'"

"And a zapper is . . . ?"

"A device the vampire hunters came up with to mess with our heads. We've developed some immunity to it, and massive amounts of pain-killers can block the effects too, but—"

"I can give you massive amounts of painkill-ers," Rose interrupted. "If they brought my fur coat, she added, looking toward the closet door.

Tony let her go. "Please say you have some-thing stronger than aspirin—"

"I've got a stash of Vicodin."

"Well, aren't you the modern movie star? Is an entourage going to show up any moment now?"

"I'd rather somebody showed up with a meal. I'm starving."

Rose didn't explain that she'd been saving the hidden medication for a suicide attempt. She didn't want to upset him. She laughed with relief when she found that the coat and all her other clothes was in this closet. She prayed that nobody had searched the pockets, and whooped with joy when her hand closed around her hidden treasure.

Tony was standing right behind her with his hands cupped when she turned around. *This is too good to be true!* he thought as he gulped down the Vicodin.

My thought, exactly, she responded.

Who cares? He added.

He swung her up into his arms and headed toward the bed. "I'm going to make love to you now," he told her firmly. "And this time we will *not* be interrupted."

Rose pressed her head to his chest and kissed the place over his heart. She put her arms around his neck and held on tight, breathing him in, never wanting to let him go. "I promise the only screaming I'll do this time will be with pleasure."

"Then you're going to be screaming a lot," he promised.

Chapter Fifty-one

December 19, 3:00 AM
Outside Los Angeles, CA

Have you ever seen werewolf CAT scans or MRI images? Sid asked Joe telepathically.

No, the black wolf loping beside her across the barren field answered. *Shh.*

Sid backed away a few feet and kept her telepathic shields tightly closed while Joe worked.

He stopped, lifted his head to taste the air, and shifted their course slightly when he padded forward again.

They'd left her SUV on the side of a gravel road a few miles back to cut across country on foot and paw. Joe'd shed his clothes for wolf form, and she'd brought a small shoulder bag stuffed with useful supplies. The night was clear, the moon was bright, but they had no trouble moving silently from shadow to shadow. The game was afoot, so to speak, and their partnership was working as smoothly as ever. Sid was almost giddy with the pleasure of being with Joe like this. Maybe nothing was settled between them, but she had this time with him to treasure.

Have you? he asked after they'd walked in silence for a while. *Seen them?* he prompted.

It took her a moment to recall the thread of the conversation. *I have indeed seen images of werewolf and other werefolk skulls.*

Why would you want to?

I was hanging out at the clinic when I was pregnant with Charles. I got bored between tests and wandered into one of the research labs, and I ran into a researcher dying to talk to somebody about her work.

And this research proved conclusively that werewolves are sexier and more glamorous than vampires.

I already knew that. Her interest was in your sense of smell. She had images of werewolf heads in human and transformed states. Guess what?

You tell me.

Werewolves in human form have the same olfactory organs as mortals. Considering that you have a superior sense of smell when you're in hu-

man shape, she believes that what you think of as
scent is actually your way of defining a psychic
sense.

Well, duh . . .

Apparently werewolves already know that
about themselves.

*Of course we do, but scientific proof is always
a good thing. As long as the information stays
where it should.*

Anthony Crowe is head of the clinic's security,
Sid defended her sire. *He's vetted everyone who
works there. Nothing gets past him.*

Except small explosive devices, and missing
little old ladies.

Joseph—

What else have Dr. C.'s mortal researchers
come up with recently? DNA studies? New super-
drugs? What sort of experiments are your mortals
doing on our people?

A great deal of suspicion flowed from Joe with
the thoughts, and she hated the implications.
*Your boy Tobias suspects that our mortal cousins
are traitors.*

They're not my cousins, my vampire darling.

He'd called her *darling*, which didn't stop her
from arguing with him. She welcomed communication with Joe no matter what they were talking
about. The last thing she wanted was for him to

return to the angry silence of a few days before, now that she'd told him the whole truth.

You can't possibly suspect everyone, can you? Sid asked.

Guilty until proven innocent is the best policy with mortals. You vampires have created this security risk, you know, by reproducing with mortals like werebunnies.

There is no such thing as werebunnies.

You take the daylight drugs; they make you more like mortals; that makes it easier for you to have kids with them.

Laurent wasn't taking daylight drugs when he got Eden knocked up, and they weren't even bonded then. Hell, they weren't even friends! Having Toni was a happy accident. Babies just— happen.

Charles didn't.

For a moment, the ache to hold her baby stopped her in her tracks.

Charles is fine, she thought. *Everything is fine.*

The voice in her mind was hers, but it seemed to come from a distance.

Are you all right, Sid?

Everything's all right.

Joe stopped at a thick tree trunk and turned into human shape. "Your turn," he told her.

Sid was glad of the chance to do something for

the case. She closed her eyes, cleared her mind, and thought of Rose. Dear, sweet, gentle, elderly Rose Cam—

Sid's entire being turned to flame, and the rush of lust drove her to her knees. Everything was fire. Everything was need. There was nothing but desire, and she reached for the naked man beside her.

Chapter Fifty-two

Joe was barely able to keep from shouting in surprise when Sid pulled him down beside her. The scent of damp earth and old pine needles did nothing to mask the powerful aroma of arousal boiling around Sidonie.

"What are you—"

Her roving hands soon showed him exactly what she intended. She knew how every part of him responded to every touch. Her caresses weren't gentle, but they were perfect. His body responded with quick arousal.

The woman could have made him come in a few moments, if he didn't fight the rising sensation.

"Honey, sweetheart, we can't—"

She seemed to have suddenly gone mad with desire. Under other circumstances he would have been happy to go along for the ride.

Her mouth covered his, her tongue twisted with his, and for a moment he matched her hunger for hunger. It took more than superhuman effort to pull away, to hold her back. He wanted to devour and be devoured, but he held on to sanity instead.

"Sid, sweetheart, stop."

She slipped out of his grasp and pressed her body to his. A strand of her hair brushed across his chest, and this simple touch sent more heat through him than anything else she'd done. He didn't want her to stop. His hands roamed over her back; and he discovered that he'd pulled up her shirt so that his palms were pressed against warm skin.

"We can do this later. Somewhere with a bed and—"

He gasped at the pressure of sharp teeth just above his left nipple.

Words obviously meant nothing to her, but he kept trying.

"We're close to the enemy. This isn't the time, and Rose—"

"Rose!"

The word came out as a gasp of hunger, and she was on him again. Joe ended up on his back, with Sid on top of him.

This time when she kissed him, Joe couldn't stop kissing back. Even as his hands moved over her without conscious will, his mind made the effort to touch her thoughts, to calm—

Big mistake.

Their minds touched, blended. There was a moment of utter clarity, sharing, understanding. A moment that lasted no more than a nanosecond, before Joe, too, went up in flames.

They tumbled around on the soft pine needles in a frantic, straining heap. He was already naked and hard. Sid's clothing took him only a moment to push aside. Joe entered her in a deep, brutal thrust. She responded with a fierce growl deep in her throat that brought an answering snarl from him. Her thighs wrapped around his hips, rising to meet his thrusts, drawing his hardness deeper into her sweet heat as he claimed his mate.

His world exploded in total completion when her teeth sank into his shoulder. His mate had claimed him.

Sid lay on her back, stared at the stars through the tree branches, and remembered how to breathe.

She was aware of who they were, and that she was utterly, happily, complete, but everything else was a blur. Joe was collapsed on top of her, keeping her warm in the cool darkness. For a long time she combed her fingers through his hair, drawing deep pleasure from this simple gesture.

"What the hell was that all about?" she finally asked.

"Uh . . . ," came Joe's muffled reply. "Shouldn't I be asking you?"

"I have no memory of anything but great sex."

"Try."

Sid watched the moon and searched her mind. "I recall your asking me to look for Rose. I let down my shields, trying to find the rose colors that reached me before . . . but what I got was . . ."

"Turned on," he supplied.

"*Somebody* was, and I don't think it was me—not initially. I think I tapped in to somebody's libido." She realized that she also had a fading headache. She found her bag on the ground by her head and rummaged around for the container of painkillers to dull the distant security device's effects.

"And?" Joe prompted.

"I reached through a zapper into a couple of very active libidos—*oh!*" She sat up, pushing Joe off of her. "Oh, dear."

"What's wrong?"

"I've never been so embarrassed in my life. That was Rose and my—no, I'm not going to even think about it." She got to her feet and pulled her partner up after her. "My apologies for attacking you like that."

He grinned and rubbed his shoulder. "No problem."

Sid looked closely at his shoulder. "Damn! I bit you again! I am so sorry—I shouldn't—"

"I liked it."

"Of course you did! But it was wrong. I had no self-control and—"

"Get over it," Joe said. "Suck it up and get it together. We're not far from our objective."

She was half tempted to salute at his brisk tone. Instead, she nodded and rearranged her bunched clothing.

Then she took Joe's hand. "We'll find Rose," she said. "But first you're going to tell me what you know about Charles."

Chapter Fifty-three

Uh-oh.

"Charles? What about Charles?"

"You couldn't sound innocent to save your life, Joseph Bleythin."

She was right; he was no good at lying and never had been. A gift for prevarication was one of the things she brought to the team.

"How does your son come into this?" he asked, genuinely puzzled. Then he recalled. "You were in my head!"

"Not on purpose and you know it, so don't sound so accusing. I didn't mean to pick up your concern about Charles. Only the concern wasn't about him, was it? What do you know about my son—about me—that I don't?"

"I've got lots of information in my head; lots of trivia, lots of classified stuff. Why'd you pick up on that bit about your kid? Oh, right, because we'd been discussing children earlier." Joe rubbed his jaw with his free hand. Sid's grip on his other wrist was like iron, a not at all subtle way of reminding him which species was on top of the food chain. "You've got me in a wolf trap, darling, and I know it. But there are some things I can't tell you."

She released his wrist and turned her back to him. "I know what I did to you was wrong. Wanting revenge is fine, but keep my son out of—"

"I don't want revenge." A couple of days ago, yes. But now: "I promised Tony not to tell you." He took Sid's shoulders and turned her gently to face him. Her assumption that he wanted to hurt her stung him, but he understood it.

"I'll relish your pain some other time, okay? But I wouldn't use Charles to hurt you. All you picked up on was some info Tony gave me."

He couldn't help but smile faintly at the puzzled look she gave him. "What's Tony got to do with Charles?"

"What specifically did you pick up from my thoughts?"

He waited patiently while she got her own thoughts in order.

"I sensed something that you didn't like—something about the way Charles is being raised. Something secret from me . . ."

Joe nodded. "I promised not to tell you, and I was assured that it's for your own good. But you're right, I don't like it."

He tried to keep his opinions to himself, tried to find a way to skirt the issue—but, damn it, he *hated* what the vampires had done to one of their own!

"I know your kind has to raise your sons differently than our wolf packs do, but this Severing custom sucks."

"Why? It's just a party before we send a two-year-old away to the Clan crèche."

Joe shook his head. "It's a telepathic severing of a mother from her son," he told her bluntly. "Your thoughts and memories were altered by your loving Clan to keep you from missing Charles. I was told that it was done so that you can live in the outside world without going crazy from an instinctive need to care for your child. It was done for your own good."

Bitterness at what she'd done to him *for his own good* crept into his voice, but anger for her burned away his lingering resentment. He hated what had been done to Sid even more than having his own memories stripped by her. Vampires spent altogether too much time making high-handed decisions about what other people should do, feel, want, think, and believe—even if it was all done with the best of intentions.

"You can't miss Charles because they've used mind control on you." She was looking very thoughtful. "Do you understand?"

"Charles is safe in the crèche," she answered. "That's what's most important."

She didn't sound like an automaton; she sounded perfectly reasonable and sincere. And that worried him. "What are you up to?" he asked.

"It's true," she said.

"Maybe it is, but I know you're up to something. I can smell it."

She stroked his cheek. "You knsow me too well, Joe." She glanced past his shoulder. "There's a place over the next hill where bad guys are holding Rose Cameron and Tony prisoner. They need rescuing, and that's what we're going to do right now."

"One thing at a time," he agreed.

Sid set off at vampire speed. Joe changed back to wolf form and loped after her.

Chapter Fifty-four

We're upwind and I've got a vampire with me, so I think we're safe from mental and physical detection. At least until sunrise, when they can see us moving across the open field.

"We'll get it done before then," Sid answered Joe's thoughts.

He'd returned to where she waited in the trees after making a quick recon of the bad guys' property. Rose was being held in a big four-story house surrounded by open ground.

Heardfelt anything else from the prisoners? Joe asked.

No. Thank goodness. The last thing she wanted was another blast of over-the-top lust.

Business now, pleasure later. *What's the layout?
Disposition of guards?*

You ought to come to work for the Dark Angels.

Sid had a moment's fantasy of running off
with Joe to live and love in secret while fighting
the good fight with his special forces team.

"Yeah, right," she said.

*I counted two mortals with guns and three fe-
rals patrolling the grounds. Lots of activity—stuff
being brought out and loaded into vans. I get the
impression that this is a temporary safe house and
they're planning on leaving real soon.*

*Then it's a good thing we didn't arrive late for
the party.* "How do you want to do this?" Sid
asked.

Joe's lips pulled back, showing a muzzle full of
razor-sharp teeth. He growled low in his throat.

"You really hate feral werewolves, don't you?"

Somehow the werewolf managed to laugh
evilly.

"I'll take the mortals, then. You take the bit
boys." She couldn't resist ruffling the fur on his
head before setting off. This brought another
growl, but no matter how fierce Joe Bleythin
could be, he never intimidated her.

"Have fun storming the castle, darling," she
told him.

Don't get dead, he thought back.

One of the many things they shared was a love of movies, and they were always quoting them to each other. Saving a movie star really was the perfect job for them.

"Well, that was certainly—"

"Invigorating?" Tony suggested as he ran a finger slowly from the base of Rose's throat all the way down to her belly button. She was lying on her back, her head propped up on pillows. He was stretched out on his side next to her. Her eyes were heavy lidded, her skin still flushed and glowing with a faint sheen of sex sweat. "You look incredibly decadent," he told her.

"I was about to say that what we've been up to was certainly distracting."

"Distracting?" he asked in mock outrage. "Young lady, do you think that I would stoop to making love to you as mere distraction?"

Her hand came up to stroke his cheek. "Oh, no," she answered with an exaggerated flutter of eyelashes. "You'd never try to get a scared woman's mind off of impending doom and disaster in such an ungentlemanly fashion."

He wiggled his eyebrows. "It worked, didn't it? You want to do it again?"

"Oh, yes. But not just yet."

"Aw . . ."

"I also noticed that we shared quite a bit of blood along with other bodily fluids. It was . . . beyond amazing."

He gave a one-shoulder shrug. "It's the vampire way."

"It was wonderful." Rose wriggled away from him and got out of bed. "Can I ask you something?" she asked after she'd pulled a nightgown on over her head.

"Can I stop you from asking?" He sat up and watched as she picked up a brush and began working tangles out of her coppery hair. He noticed that she didn't turn toward any mirrors to help with the job. He held out his hand. "Come here and let me do that for you."

Rose sat beside him and gave him the heavy ivory brush. "That's nice," she said as he stroked the soft bristles gently through her hair.

She was silent for a while, and Tony hoped he'd escaped a coming inquisition. But he'd only delayed her curiosity for a while.

"You were lying about my restored youth being your doing, weren't you?" She shifted on the bed to face him. The fear was back in her eyes, but her jaw was set stubbornly.

He couldn't lie to her this time. "It was a strong supposition on my part. Blood sharing in a bond causes mortals' bodies to stay young. Bondmates age together, slowly."

"But sharing blood doesn't make old bondmates young again, does it?"

"I don't know," he admitted. "I hope so. Why not? I don't think it's ever been tried before." He grinned. "We can be the first."

"You are an impractical romantic and always have been." She smiled. "And I love you for it." But the fear hadn't left her eyes.

He took her hands and kissed them. "You want to go somewhere and get a bite to eat?"

"I'd love to," she said. She tilted her head toward the door. "I think we have a slight problem, though."

"Why use a door when a window will do?" He stood and urged her to her feet.

"But—there are bars on the window. And guards outside."

Even with her youth restored, Rose's mortal hearing was no match for his. A pity, because she was missing a minor, if muffled, riot in the distance. "We don't have to worry about the guards. My daughter's finally joined the party." He led her toward the window.

Rose balked. "You have a daughter?"

He nodded. "And she brought her werewolf boyfriend."

"You have a daughter," Rose repeated. She looked toward the window. "And she's come to rescue us?"

"Hell, no," he replied with a wild grin. "I'm the rescuer. Sid and Joe are creating a diversion."

With that, he wrapped her bathrobe around his hands, broke the window glass, and quickly studied the last barrier blocking the way out. What Rose had referred to as bars was actually a less conspicuous heavy mesh barrier.

"This chicken wire is silver—nice touch on their part." His skin warmed at the touch of silver even through the cloth. Normally the daylight drugs in his system would have combated the silver allergy, but he guessed whatever antivamp potion the mad scientists had pumped into him still had a lingering effect.

"Be careful," she said.

"It won't burn through before I'm done," he told her as he twisted and worked at the metal.

Silver was harder for a vampire to bend than steel, but Tony didn't let a little thing like that stop him, not with the woman he loved watching him. It was his duty to be her hero. It took him a while, and every muscle in his body ached by the time the silver mesh dropped to the ground.

"Time to go, sweetheart." He turned back to Rose and held out his hand.

To his shock, she was standing with her back against the door, her palms pressed flat against it. She stared at the opening he'd made for her to the outside world, her indigo eyes huge with terror.

"I can't go out there," she said. "I can't."

Chapter Fifty-five

"For crying out loud, woman! Now what is your problem?"

Anthony's anger brought Rose somewhat out of the paralyzing terror. "Well, excuse me for having a few issues, Mr. Perfect Hero! I haven't been outside of this room—or one just like it—in years. Years!"

"Don't tell me that you're scared of the outside world."

"Precisely."

"This from the woman who faced down a German tank?"

"That was 1944. I belonged in that time . . .

but now . . . Anthony, I'm a dinosaur. I barely know what the Internet is. I—"

He stalked across the room to lean his palms flat against the door on either side of her head. His long, naked length pressed against her as he brought his face close to hers. "You've been given the chance to live again. I don't believe that you're too much of a coward not to grab on to that chance and discover a new life. But you're the only one who can make the decision to step out into the world." He gave her his most charming smile. "What's it going to be: me and happily ever after? Or are you going to take your chances with a bunch of mad scientists?"

She sighed. She wanted to be with him more than anything—even if it meant stepping out into a strange world where the only thing she had to rely on was his love. And that, come to think of it, was quite a lot for her to hold on to.

"Are you going to pick me up and jump out the window if I decide to go with the scientists?"

"You bet I am."

Rose put her arms around Anthony's neck. She'd been afraid plenty of times in her life, and the only way to handle it was to do what had to be done.

"All right, we're going out the window. But not until you put some clothes on."

* * *

Sid's head hurt and she didn't like the smell of fresh blood, but she fought off the temptation to inform Joe that killing wasn't always the answer, no matter how much pleasure it might give him.

Werewolves fought each other to the death; it was not her place as a vampire to complain or condemn. She was careful not to watch the business Joe was about behind her as she silently moved toward the mortals that were her targets.

She could smell the men at the back of the house because they wore the bulbs of garlic that the most fanatical Purists still used as an antivampire talisman. It must be an almost religious custom, because the vampire hunters knew very well that most vampires took drugs that made them immune to the old curses.

"It's a waste of a perfectly good member of the onion family if you ask me," she muttered as she approached her first target.

He heard her and whirled around, bringing up a rifle as he moved.

"Make pasta sauce, not war," Sid said as she ripped the weapon from his hands.

He was unconscious before he had a chance to make any noise, and she secured his wrists and ankles with a flex cuff from her pack. She made equally quick work of the second mortal, then paused on one knee to examine one of the weapons she'd confiscated. She wasn't pleased to find that the rifle had been modified to fire bullets containing substances toxic to her kind—silver, garlic, and hawthorn wood.

"Bastards," she muttered.

Purists really did make it hard to believe that most mortals were perfectly nice people. As she started to stand, her attention was caught by movement at the top floor, and she smiled. A male figure dropped to the ground, took a few steps back, and held up his arms. A few seconds later, a figure in a white nightgown leapt from the fourth-floor window to be caught in the waiting male's arms.

"Rescue accomplished," Sid said.

She began to stand once more, only to crash flat onto her face when the werewolf she hadn't noticed pounced on her back. Fangs sank deeply into the back of her neck before she could throw the creature off.

Sid reared back in a moment of hideous pain, which instantly filled her veins with sexual fire. Her fingers scrabbled at the grass and she bit down hard on her tongue to stifle the scream.

Of ecstasy.

Damn it, Joseph! What do you think you're doing?

Turnabout's fair play, darling, her werewolf lover thought back.

It had been a long time since she'd known the sexual release of anyone tasting her blood. An orgasm paled in comparison with the completion calling to her now. Sid's body shook with arousal and her mind begged to give in to this pleasure like no other.

Not now, darling! Please, not now! Her mind shouted the words while her body begged for more.

"I hate it when you're right," Joe said.

Sid didn't know when he'd switched into his human shape, but at the sound of his voice she became far too aware of his naked body pressing against her.

"Please move," she said.

He shifted position and Sid rolled onto her back. His blue eyes glittered with an expression that was at once amused, aroused, and possessive. She liked the way he looked at her. She grinned up at him while she got her breathing and the rest of her responses under control.

"We have things to discuss," he said.

Sid got to her feet as she nodded. She gave Joe a hand up, making herself ignore the shiver of desire at the contact. By the time they'd turned to face the building, the two escaped prisoners had reached them, holding hands.

Sid stared at the strangely familiar young woman, then at her sire. "Tony, why are you wearing a pink bathrobe?"

Chapter Fifty-six

"Because Rose insisted that people don't run around outdoors naked."

Rose was all too aware of her beloved Anthony's sarcasm as she tried not to stare at the nude male standing beside the young blond woman. She, at least, was clothed. Rose breathed in the fresh night air and remembered that not only was she a fair actress, but that once upon a time she'd enjoyed interacting with other people. Time to renew old habits.

"Thank you for your assistance," she said to the woman. Curiosity got the better of her. "Anthony called you his daughter . . . ?"

"This is Sidonie Wolf." Anthony's glance moved

suspiciously between the other couple for a few moments, his eyes narrowed. "And this is her—bondmate?—Joe Bleythin." He did not sound the least bit pleased at what he'd said.

"Uh—" naked Joe began.

"You *are* Rose Cameron! Aren't you?" Sidonie said.

Rose nodded. Fear that the young woman would respond with revulsion knotted her stomach.

"Wow," said Joe. There was nothing but awed appreciation in his tone. "You're a movie star."

"And he's a werewolf," Anthony said. "Who's somehow attached to my daughter," he added grumpily.

The vampire female reached out to touch her but stopped at Rose's automatic flinch. Sidonie turned her attention to Anthony. "How—"

"Long story," he cut her off. He jerked a thumb over his shoulder at the building. "No one's noticed our absence yet, and it's time to go."

"I couldn't agree more. Anthony, what are you doing?" Rose asked as he swung her up in his arms.

"We'll travel faster if I carry you."

Good Lord, it was the Ardennes all over again! "My ankle's fine and I have no intention of living in the past. Put me down, Anthony Crowe." He responded so quickly that he almost dropped her, but at least she was on her feet. "You have a car waiting somewhere, I take it?" she asked when she was standing upright. "Please tell me that you didn't bring a tank this time."

He chuckled. "Well, it is a Hummer. I left it parked half a mile from here."

"You two get going," Joe said. "Sid and I will cover your withdrawal." He tapped his forehead. "I've already called in reinforcements from the Dark Angels."

"When did you do that?" Sidonie asked.

"I reported back just before we ran into zapper interference."

It all sounded terribly military and interesting to Rose, but before she could ask for any explanations, Anthony put his arm around her waist and said, "Come on—we're getting out of here."

After Tony and his hot teenage girlfriend were gone, Sid turned to Joe with her arms crossed and anger in every line of her body. "And just why do you think we need help from your precious Dark Angels?"

"I'm following standard procedure. What are you annoyed about?"

"I do not need any help in securing this objective—or whatever military term you want to use."

The reason for her attitude began to dawn on

Joe. She thought he was treating her like a *girl,* the way the males of her own kind would. As if he ever would—although the thought of treating her like an incredibly sexy woman whenever the opportunity arose was appealing.

"Of course you don't need help," he told her. "I'm not disputing that you're the big bad vampire and can rip everyone in that house to shreds with a dirty look. But I thought your only objective was to rescue Rose Cameron. The Angels' assignment is to take down the whole conspiracy her kidnapping was part of, so I called them in."

The explanation mollified her somewhat. "That's lame," she said. "But I'll let it go because we have something far more important to talk about. You're biting me was wonderful, but the complications are—"

"Shouldn't we kick some ass before we get into that?" he interrupted.

Sid frowned but went along with the distraction. "Don't you think that's interfering with your Dark Angels assignment?"

He shrugged. "Yeah, but it'll be fun."

They started toward the house. "Don't kill anyone you don't have to," Sid advised.

* * *

Once the house was secured, they waited on the front porch. Sid had moved the guards she'd cuffed earlier in to join the two mortals they'd left secured in the cell on the fourth floor. There'd been no supernatural bad guys inside. After shutting off the zapper, they'd made a thorough search of the house and grounds. Nobody and nothing else was found. Sid had considered questioning the prisoners, but Joe wanted to wait for the Dark Angels to show up.

She'd shrugged and said, "Sure. My work here is done anyway."

He'd gone back to her SUV to retrieve his clothes, which she found mildly disappointing, but he'd declared he was cold just sitting around. So now they waited, seated side by side on the porch steps while dawn lightened the sky. The rising sun brought a little warmth into the frigid air.

After a long silence, Joe yawned and stretched. "Is it Christmas yet?"

It really wasn't a holiday Sid paid much attention to. "Not for a few days, I think."

"It was a rhetorical question."

She sighed. "Sorry. I think I'm too tired for rhetoric." She sighed again. "We need to talk, though."

Joe put his arm around her shoulders and she relaxed against his long, lean form. "Yeah."

Silence stretched out between them for a long time after this acknowledgment.

Finally, Joe said, "I can still taste you—feel you—inside of me."

Sid waited, holding her breath.

"And I like it," he told her reluctantly. "I guess I never understood before what sharing blood really meant to you. I still don't understand, but I feel it. As a hunter, I thought I understood the taste of blood. I've taken prey in wolf form—rabbits, deer, wild boar—I've known the chase and the kill and the feeding. I've tasted the death of the werewolves I've brought down. But this give and take, this sharing and becoming one, that's the essence of . . ."

"Bonding," Sid said when it seemed that Joe couldn't form that word.

"I bit you because you've bitten me." He squeezed her shoulder. "I realize now how stupid and childish and dangerous and wonderful it was. Especially wonderful. I've tasted you once; I want to do it again. The werewolf part of me doesn't understand this need at all."

"I'm sorry," Sid told him. "Maybe it'll wear off."

"Do you want it to wear off?"

"Hell no. I just don't want to get you in trouble. And what do you mean, *the werewolf part* of you? What part of you isn't werewolf?"

"I know I'm not defining it correctly. Maybe there's a part of me now that's vampire."

Sid grunted. "Not likely. Do you think that your biting me will turn me into a werewolf?"

"I doubt vampires can be turned." He ran his hand through her hair. "You'd make a cute golden werewolf, though."

A large black SUV turned into the long driveway then, so they put the conversation aside and stood to await the arrival of the Dark Angels. But when the vehicle stopped, three Primes got out; it was Sid's cousin Kiril and a pair of Shagal vampires. They all wore grim expressions as they approached her and Joe.

Kiril made a formal bow to her. "Lady Sidonie: for you, from Lady Juanita." He handed her a small red velvet bag.

Sid felt the weight of the object inside the bag and knew exactly what it was. "Damn," she muttered.

She spilled the bag's contents into her palm, and sure enough, it was a ruby ring, the symbol of Lady Juanita's authority as the Matri of Clan Wolf. It meant that the Matri wanted to see Sidonie *right now*. There was no ignoring this summons.

Sid squeezed the ring in her fist. "Of course," she said to Kiril. "I want to discuss a matter of importance with her anyway. I'll leave for San Diego immediately."

"She's not in San Diego," Kiril answered. "She's at the Shagal Citadel." He gestured toward the SUV. "Please come with us."

"The werewolf comes as well," one of the Shagal Primes said.

Oh, goddess, she'd been afraid of this! "That won't be necessary. He's waiting to report to the Dark Angel commander."

"Lady Serisa commands that the werewolf accompany you," the Prime answered.

"But—" Kiril began.

"Of course I'm coming," Joe announced. His arm went around her shoulders again and he looked calmly at the trio of glaring Primes. "Let's get this over with, shall we?"

Sid didn't want to get it over with; she was terrified that at the end of the upcoming meeting, Joe Bleythin would be dead—punished for her crime.

She was so sorry. So very sorry. But he insisted on being brave and there was nothing she could do but love him for it.

Chapter Fifty-seven

December 19, 10:00 AM
Vampire Medical Clinic
Los Angeles, CA

Rose frowned at the Band-Aid covering the inside crook of her elbow and flexed her arm. The needle hadn't hurt going in, but she hated Anthony and his doctor friends' insistence on yet more medical testing. They'd taken three tubes of blood before she'd pointed out that a vampire's girlfriend really didn't have that much to spare, and the tech had agreed to leave her alone for a while.

"I spent at least a year as a guinea pig," she'd complained.

"We're going to make absolutely certain you're not being used as one now," the mortal in charge—Dr. Casmerek—insisted. He had a kind smile to go along with a no-nonsense demeanor. "We're going to make sure you stay as young and healthy as you are now."

He was very sincere, and he talked a good game. Besides, Anthony trusted him. So Rose held out her arm and let them take her blood. She knew they had a whole battery of other procedures planned as well, but not right now. She was determined about that.

"I want strong black coffee," she said as the examination room door opened and Anthony walked in. "And all the cholesterol I can get—although knowing the way people eat in this town, finding fried, greasy food might prove a hardship."

Anthony smiled lovingly at her. "You know I'll provide you with anything you want."

She didn't know if she wanted this *Your wish is my command* business to last. That was no way to run a relationship, but she decided to go along with it for now.

"You look gorgeous," she told him.

He posed for her, holding out his arms and turning around slowly. He'd shed her pink robe for an ensemble of black, black, and more black—shirt, slacks, jacket, tie, shoes. The clothes fit the way only expensive tailoring could.

"Armani?" Rose asked.

"The designer of choice for well-dressed vampires," Anthony acknowledged. "Since I run security here, I have a room and a well-stocked closet on the premises." He set a large bag from an upscale department store down beside her. "To provide your wardrobe, I had to go out shopping."

Rose almost squealed with delight as she snatched up the bag. "Merry Christmas to me!" She spilled the contents out on the examining table, then picked up the pieces one by one. "Underwear! Thank God, you brought me a bra!" She exclaimed over every piece of clothing as she found it, and when she was done looking she let Anthony help her put it on.

"Everything fits," she said when she was dressed in a linen skirt and silk knit tunic. She wiggled her toes in the black leather sandals. "Even the shoes."

"I guessed at your sizes from memory." He ran his hands over her from shoulders to hips. "Tactile memory," he added, then took her arm. "Let me show you our garden, Rose."

"I'm delighted to get out of any place that contains medical equipment," she answered.

Outside, Rose turned her face up to the sky and breathed in air rich with—

"Bacon! And coffee!" She gave Anthony a look of surprised delight. "You're wonderful!"

"So I am. So is the staff here at the clinic. Right this way, young lady." Anthony led her to a small wooden table set for two and pulled out a chair for her. "I thought you might like breakfast alfresco."

Rose's stomach rumbled. She kissed his cheek before he went to sit opposite her. "I'll take breakfast any way I can get it."

Anthony poured coffee for her into a china cup, then whisked the cover off a plate full of all the bad-for-her food she could possibly want. Rose dug in with the gusto of—well, of a teenager.

"You do know that Dr. Casmerek thinks you're robbing the cradle with me," Rose said between bites of toast she'd covered with scrambled egg.

"He's just jealous." Anthony sipped coffee. "Tell me about Gregor," he said after she was half-done with her meal.

By then, Rose was ready to slow down enough to savor the flavors and textures of her food while they talked.

She gazed at Anthony, so perfectly groomed, so handsome, so seemingly relaxed. So very angry beneath the polished exterior. Rose sighed romantically. "How I do love a dangerous man."

He frowned. "Gregor?"

She laughed at his jealousy. "No, you." She sat

back, coffee cup in one hand, a triangle of toast in the other. "Give me a moment to get my memories in order."

She'd been used to memorizing scripts for film and stage, and she hadn't lost a bit of her mental acuity over the years. It didn't take her long before she was able to repeat almost verbatim her conversation with Gregor while she was being held prisoner.

"I assume he wanted all of that information conveyed to somebody, or he wouldn't have told me all the plans of the Tribe vampires," she concluded. "I don't think real-life villains really spill their evil plans while gloating over their prisoners."

"You think he isn't a villain?"

"I've been in pain for a long time because of him. I think he's a sadistic bastard." A vision of the handsome Tribe Prime formed in her mind, and she wanted to spit into that perfect face. "But I also think he arranged our escape for some reason and provided information he wants you to know about."

Anthony nodded. "I concur." He rubbed his jaw. "No doubt he was sowing lies and working plans within plans. It will all be checked out and—"

"Tony! Tony, I'm so glad I found you!"

Anthony stood and Rose turned to look as a frantic young man hurried toward them. He was big and blond and very handsome. Rose figured he was another Prime. Dr. Casmerek followed after him.

"What's wrong now, Kiril?" Anthony asked.

The Prime stopped in front of him. "It's Lady Sidonie. She's in a lot of trouble—and it's all my fault!"

Chapter Fifty-eight

Shagal Citadel

Sid protested when she and Joe were separated upon entering the Citadel, but no one listened to her. She wasn't used to being ignored by Primes, but Joe looked back and said, "Let it go, Sidonie," as he was led away. His warning to keep her cool kept her from having a screaming tantrum. Tantrums were not normally her way, but fear for Joe's safety drove her to the brink.

She kept reminding herself that they'd shared enough blood and their souls were entwined enough that if anything happened to him she would know it. This didn't keep her from pacing the room they'd put her in, her arms wrapped around herself in fear, but she managed not to break anything or try to escape.

The Matri demanded my presence. I have no choice but to await the Matri's pleasure.

Sid repeated the mantra constantly. It didn't help that they'd also taken her cell phone from her, and that there were too many telepathic shields guarding the Shagal Citadel for her to call out in a psychic way.

She was stuck in another Clan's territory without a clue and feeling helpless.

"Which is just what they want," she muttered after an endless amount of pacing. "They're trying to break me."

The door opened and a Shagal Prime looked at her. With no expression on his face or in his voice, he said, "You will come with me."

"Fine."

Sid didn't follow him, but led the way to the Citadel's windowless central meeting room. She waited for the Prime to enter first and announce, "Sidonie Wolf as you commanded, my ladies."

Sid tightened her mental shields and schooled her features to absolute blankness as she stepped inside, only to have her barriers explode in surprise when she saw how many Matris were waiting for her.

There was Lady Serisa Shagal, of course, mistress of the Citadel. Lady Juanita occupied a deep leather chair beside Serisa. Seated on a couch were Lady Angelica Reynard and Lady Cassandra Crowe. Sid also recognized the Matris of the Snake and Wolverine Clans, though she didn't know those women.

Why were they all here? Why were they staring at her? This was a gathering of the Furies, wasn't it? Oh, Lady, this was going to be bad.

Sid acted as if there was no one else in the room but her own Clan Matri. She put the Matri's ruby ring into Juanita's outstretched hand before she stepped back, planted herself in front of Lady Juanita's chair, and said, "I want my baby back."

"We are not gathered to discuss Charles," Juanita replied.

"I am. My son is my only concern. You know my rights, Lady Juanita. I have provided my Clan with a child. I am head of House Sidonie. My child is *mine*."

Cassandra Crowe responded, "Nicely played, Sid, going on the offensive to throw us off track, but we aren't going to discuss a child who's safely in your Clan crèche."

"It is your illicit relationship with the werewolf that's the problem," Lady Serisa said.

"What problem?" Joe asked.

Sid had known when he came in the door behind her, but she'd kept her attention on Juanita. Now she turned to him and said, "Yeah, what problem?"

His warm smile told her everything she needed to know about how he felt about her, about his forgiveness, about their love and partnership.

"I don't see any problem," they said together.

Vampire Medical Clinic

The sunny garden seemed to fill with shadows around Anthony. "What's happened?"

"The werewolf," Kiril answered.

"I knew Joe was going to get her into trouble."

Rose stepped to Anthony's side, and he took her hand. "Isn't Joe the naked young man who helped to rescue us?"

"Lady Juanita sent for Sidonie because of the werewolf," Kiril explained. "It is right and proper for the Matri to discourage such involvement. But the Shagal Primes made the werewolf go to the Citadel with them as well, and it wasn't a friendly request." The young man looked devastated. "I didn't mean to put their lives in danger when I reported seeing them together. They've convened a meeting of Matris to judge them—to condemn him."

"This is bad." Dr. Casmerek twisted his hands together. "I hate it when vampire biology overcomes civilized behavior."

"How bad?" Rose asked, only to be ignored.

"I'd hoped it wouldn't go this far." Anthony shook his head. "Poor Sidonie. She's going to take losing him very hard. And poor Joe Bleythin. That boy's likely to be a spot of bloody fur by the time this is done."

Fear shot through Rose and she squeezed Anthony's hand as hard as she could. "Talk to me!" she demanded. "What is going on? Why would you say something so awful about Joe?"

"Vampire females aren't allowed to bond with anyone but Primes," he explained. "It is forbidden by ancient custom and law."

"Why?" Rose asked.

"Because—"

"Did obeying ancient custom and law do you any good?" she asked. "Or me? Us? I saw those two together—they're in love. What's wrong with that?"

"The Matris rule and—"

"Joe was there to help us. You can't stand aside and let him be killed for no good reason."

"Executed," Anthony corrected. "It's not the

same thing as a simple killing. There's no way—"

"Is Sid your daughter?"

"I'm her sire, but there's nothing I can do to—"

"Do you love her?"

Anthony looked stricken by her questions. She watched intently while his warring emotions flashed across his face.

She finally twisted the knife. "Are you going to let anyone hurt your little girl?" She knew very well that he was aware of the unspoken end of her sentence: *the way you hurt me.*

"You fight dirty, love of my life."

Rose nodded. She also didn't have to add that her wish was his command. "Help Sid," she said. "You won't forgive yourself if you don't try."

Anthony ran a hand through his hair, and his stricken expression turned thoughtful. "There is someone who can help. Maybe. Come on," he told Kiril.

"Where to?" the other Prime asked.

"To find Tobias Strahan. He's not going to let anything happen to one of his Dark Angels."

"No man left behind?" Kiril asked. "Would the Angels rebel against the Matris over one life?"

"We can hope so," Anthony said.

"By the goddess, what have I started?" the worried young Prime asked.

"Vampire bonding with werewolf," Dr. Casmerek said thoughtfully. He nodded as if he'd come to some important decision. "I'm coming with you as well."

"Thanks, doc, but a mortal shouldn't put himself in harm's way like that."

"Braving a den of Matris? I agree, but I can help. I am coming."

"Me too!" Rose piped up. Now that she had her life back, she wasn't going to spend it sitting on her hands.

Anthony grinned at her. "Of course you are. You're never leaving my side again."

Chapter Fifty-nine

Shagal Citadel

"I love you," Sid said to Joe.

"I love you," he answered. They stood face-to-face, gazes only on each other.

"You two are not making this any easier on yourselves," Lady Juanita said. "Stop showing your defiance."

Joe turned to face the Wolf Matri. "You know that I and my pack respect your Clan," he told her. "But I'm not going to deny what I feel for Sidonie. She's tried to deny what she feels for me for years, and it's done nothing but cause her pain. Your females are precious to you—why do you want one of them in pain?"

"Because I'm nothing more than a breeding

machine to them," Sid said. All the bitterness she'd hidden for years was in her voice, and in the sneer she turned on the seated women.

"Don't be ridiculous," Serisa said, radiating disapproval.

"She's not far from being right," Lady Cassandra said. There were shocked gasps from some of the other Matri, but Cassandra spoke to Sid. "But there are many other considerations besides your breeding uses that weigh into the rules against a female bonding with anyone but a Prime."

"Such as?" Joe asked. He didn't flinch from all the glares turned his way. "You're going to kill me no matter what I say," he told the women. "I don't know why you're bothering with this trial—or whatever it is."

"Yeah, Mom," Cassie Shagal said from the doorway. "What are you trying to accomplish here?"

Everyone's attention now turned to the heir of Clan Shagal. She walked into the council room, but she didn't come alone. Several other vampire females came in with her. Joe recognized Flare Reynard, and, of course—

"Mom," Sid said to Lady Antonia Wolf. "What are you doing here?"

"Flare said you were in trouble when she called," Antonia answered, serenely smiling at

Sid. She turned that smile on the Matris. "And she mentioned something about starting the revolution. I knew I had to be in on that."

"You don't want to go in," Barak said, his tall, wide body blocking the Citadel entrance. "You really don't want to go in there."

Tony glanced from where Barak stood, at the center of a line of guardian Primes on the steps of the mansion, to the crowd he'd brought with him on the brick-paved drive.

"If my daughter isn't sent out, I'm going in." Rose tugged on his hand. "My daughter and Joseph Bleythin," he added.

"Are you holding a pack member prisoner?" Shaggy Harker asked the Prime Elder. "Do you want a war with werefolk as well as the Purists?" the Los Angeles werewolf leader demanded.

Shaggy had been with the Dark Angel leader when they'd caught up with him. Once Shaggy discovered what the problem was, he'd insisted on coming along to add his voice to the cause. Tony was aware that the situation was now way too complicated, but there was no backing off.

"If I may." Tobias Strahan stepped to the front of the crowd and looked at the opposing Primes. "I see males from more than the Shagal

Clan here. May I ask why?" His tone was mild, but he had an air of command that even Barak responded to.

"A group of Matris is holding a council inside," Barak answered. "Their Primes are here to protect them."

Tobias rubbed his jaw. "I see. You realize that this puts Lady Serisa in violation of her agreement with the Dark Angels. I'll be withdrawing my troops—although I doubt even your force of Primes can get the Matris out of this trap."

Like everyone else, Barak wasn't used to the implication that a Matri could do any wrong. "What are you talking about?"

"This territory is already under attack from the Purists," Tobias reminded Barak. "Purists who have excellent intel about vampires' current movements. They know the Matris are here. And you know what Purists do to our females."

Tony, Barak, and all the other Primes exchanged uncomfortable looks.

"I hadn't thought of that," Tony muttered.

Apparently Barak hadn't, either. "You should speak to Matri Serisa," he said to Tobias. "I'll take you to her."

"I have important information for the Matri as well," Dr. Casmerek said when Barak tried to stop him from going into the house.

"I'm head of security for the territory outside the Citadel," Tony reminded Barak.

"I speak for the werefolk," Shaggy said.

"I'm with the band?" Rose piped up.

"All right, all of you come with me," Barak said. "With the crowd already gathered in there, who's going to notice a few extra people?"

Chapter Sixty

"Revolution?" Lady Juanita asked, slowly rising to her feet.

Her attention was on Antonia, and Sid resisted the urge to move protectively to her mother's side.

"What sort of revolution do you have in mind?" Cassandra Crowe asked. This Matri's attention was on the younger females who had come to stand near Sid. "Are you showing a united front against your elders?"

"We're making a stand for our rights," Flare Reynard said.

"Rights? Oh, please!" Anjelica Reynard scoffed. She pointed at her daughter. "You're a spoiled-rotten disgrace to your Clan."

"As you have pointed out many times before." Flare put her hand on her abdomen. "I'm going to give my Clan a vampire child." She gestured at Sid. "She gave her Clan a vampire child. We're as dutiful as we can be, considering when and where we live."

"When and where?" Serisa asked. "What has that to do—"

"Twenty-first-century America," Cassie Shagal said. "It makes a big difference to our lives. We're suffocating."

"You have more freedom than we had," Cassandra pointed out.

Sid looked at Joe. "Do you think we could sneak out while this is going on?" she whispered to him.

"I heard that," Lady Juanita told her.

Sid shrugged at the Matri's stern tone. Was she supposed to apologize for bringing a little levity to her own execution?

"I want our daughters to have a freer life than I've had," Antonia said.

This turned Juanita's attention back to Sid's mother. "After the years you spent as a prisoner of the Tribes, that is understandable."

"I'm speaking of the years after I was returned to the loving, stifling bosom of my Clan," Antonia said. "I've been treated like a fragile piece of porcelain. If there's one thing being with the Tribes taught me, it is that I'm as tough as nails. I can survive anything. I want my daughter to have the freedom to find out how strong she is."

Juanita gestured at Sid. "Your daughter has had too much freedom. Look at what she's done."

"She's bonded with a werewolf," Serisa said.

"I fell in love with a mortal in my youth," Cassandra Crowe said. "I loved that man, and I love him still, but I didn't bond with him."

"A bond is a psychic link that's meant to be," Flare said. "That's what we're told all our lives. Is that just romantic drivel you feed to the Primes? Or is it the truth? Is the joining of two souls, spirits, and bodies the core of what we are?"

"Of course the bond is the most important thing to us," Serisa said.

"Then where is my crime?" Sid asked. "What have Joe and I done wrong?"

"He's a werewolf!" Serisa told her.

"The fact that they were even able to bond proves that it was meant to be," Flare argued.

"Stop and think about how prejudiced you're being, Mother," Cassie said to Serisa.

The door opened again. "My apologies for this interruption, my love," Elder Barak said as he ushered in yet another group of people, including Tony, Tobias, Shaggy, and a couple of mortals. "I am convinced that what these people have to say is important."

Serisa folded her arms and glared at the newcomers. "It had better be." Her fangs flashed as she spoke.

Tony recalled that there was a saying among vampires: *When a Matri shows fangs, bare your throat and die like a Prime.*

Either Tobias Strahan hadn't heard this saying, or he didn't care. "Matri Serisa, you are the last person on Earth I took for a fool." He made a sweeping gesture, taking in all the females in the room. "In fact, I didn't expect any *one* of you to be rash enough to walk into a war zone."

"They didn't walk, they came in limos," Flare Reynard muttered.

"If you recall," Tobias continued to Serisa, "you authorized me to put this city on lockdown. It is not our custom to call Convocations in the middle of an emergency."

Serisa stared at the Prime in shock. After a few moments of absorbing his words, she closed her eyes. "By the Lady of the Moon, I am an idiot."

Tony watched the Matris carefully, aware that they were holding a swift telepathic communication. Energy in the room buzzed and crackled, and he got the impression that the younger females were having a confab of their own.

Tobias didn't wait for the Matris to return their attention to their subjects but said loudly, "The Purists are going to find a gathering of females irresistible. Their current strategy is to try for public attacks. How do you hide this Citadel from the world when media helicopters will be flying over the place, showing the battle on news shows with live feeds?"

"Maybe this will convince them that we're living in a new age and that we have to change to cope with modern reality," Cassie said to Tobias.

"I am Prime," he answered. "My duty is to protect vampires. Creating policy is for you females."

"Oh, that's a nice one," Tony heard Sid whisper to Joe.

She was reading nuances and power plays into the situation even while she and her boyfriend were in danger, and he smiled, proud of his smart kid.

"We will close this Convocation," Lady Juanita announced.

"But what do we do about the werewolf?" Serisa demanded.

"We will reconvene after the emergency. The werewolf will be kept prisoner until—"

"The hell you say!" Shaggy shouted.

"You cannot hold one of my men, Lady Juanita," Tobias interjected. "While I and all other Primes in the Dark Angels would obey your commands, the Angels are made up of every type of supernatural being. Our policy is to protect our own. I would not order werefolk and witches and elves to stand down from storming the Citadel to rescue one of our own. They might not obey me if I did."

Tony almost looked forward to the hubbub this was going to cause as soon as the stunned Matris got their voices back.

But instead of a riot ensuing, Dr. Casmerek took the opportunity to jump in. "Ladies, Primes, werefolk," he said loudly. "There's no need for this dispute at all. No crime against either of your subspecies has been committed."

Chapter Sixty-one

"What the hell are you talking about?" Shaggy Harker asked.

The scientist had everyone's attention, and this was the first time Tony had ever seen the mortal brave enough to give Primes shots look nervous.

"What's up?" Tony asked the doctor.

Casmerek kept his attention on the Matris. "I have research findings that I've been putting off sharing with you for some time. I told myself it wasn't relevant, but I used that as an excuse because I knew you weren't going to like it."

"What is *it*?" Serisa demanded. "Cut to the chase: no scientific gobbledygook."

The mortal took a deep breath, "Okay." He pointed at Sid and Joe. "DNA testing shows that vampire/werewolf mating that resulted in the psychic talents of the Hunyara Romany tribe could only have been the genetic product of a female vampire having offspring with a male werewolf."

"What?" Serisa shouted.

"How is that possible?" Juanita asked.

"That is a perversion of everything we believe," Angelica said.

"Maybe history lies," Cassandra put in.

"Could this be true?" Serisa demanded.

"I knew you weren't going to like it," Casmerek said. "But scientific facts and history frequently don't get along. Please remember that modern vampires accept science and use it even when it contradicts folklore."

"This has happened before? We aren't the first?" Joe asked. "A werewolf and vampire bonding? Cool."

"What do you mean *cool*?" Shaggy asked. "That's—"

"Scientific fact," Casmerek put in. He took a flash drive out of his coat pocket. "I have all the data here for you to study."

Tony put his hands on Sid and Joe's shoulders. "So, no harm, no foul," he said cheerfully to the gathering. "Can we all go now?"

"We have already closed this Convocation," Juanita said. "While we still have much to discuss and decide—"

"We aren't done," Sid said. "What about Charles? I told you that I want my baby back."

"Not *now*," Tony whispered in his daughter's ear.

"You don't miss him, do you?" Tobias said to Sid. "You agree that the crèche is the safest place for a child in wartime?"

"I see your point, but—"

"The Rite of Severing was performed? The telepathic block still holds?"

"Yes!" Sid answered him angrily. "What's it to you?"

Tobias looked at the younger females before he spoke to Sid. "I need your telepathic talents. I want you to join the Dark Angels."

"Yes!" Cassie and Flare shouted, and high-fived each other.

"Do it!" Antonia urged.

Sid and Joe looked at each other for a long time, while everyone else in the crowd seemed to hold their breath and the tension between the generations grew.

"Your people need you to do this," Tobias urged quietly.

" 'Come live with me and be my love . . . ' "

Joe quoted poetry to Sid. "And we'll kick butt together."

Sid sighed deeply and gave a small nod. Then she looked to the younger females, who gave her thumbs up and grins, and a friendly but jealous glare from Flare.

Finally Sid looked at Lady Juanita. "Matri, have I your blessing?"

"Blessing?" the Wolf Clan Matri answered. "No, you do not have my blessing." She looked first at her fellow Matri, then at the younger females before returning to Sid. "You *do* have my permission."

While Sid and Joe shared a fierce hug and the younger females shouted their approval, Juanita looked at Tony. "I agree with you that everyone can go home now."

Good, Rose whispered in his mind. *All's well that ends well . . . and I really want to have sex again soon.*

Sid took a grateful breath of air when she and Joe finally stepped out into the daylight. She ignored the smells of car engines and the people moving purposefully to obey Tobias and Barak's orders to get the Matris and females out of town. She wasn't going anywhere but to a post with the Dark Angels.

Joe put his arm around her waist and pulled her close. "You look relaxed, but your scent's still scared."

She rubbed her head against his shoulder, loving his solid presence. "It'll take me a while to stop rerunning what I thought was going to happen in there," she admitted to him. She didn't mind letting him know she was scared. She was never going to lie about her emotions to him again. She didn't have to. Besides, their blood flowed as one; they *were* one. She'd almost lost this chance for completion.

"What did you think was going to happen?" he asked cautiously. "I know they wanted to kill me, but . . ."

"Kill you, yes—while I watched. Your death would have driven me mad, or killed me, too. And what happened to me would have been used as an example to keep other females from following in my wicked footsteps."

He stiffened with protective anger. "Nasty."

"We are vampires," she reminded him. "Predators use harsh measures when they have to. You know that, werewolf. And the Matris were thinking of the good of all the Clans—they would have grieved our passing. Fortunately, the Clans seem ready to change whether the Matris like it or not. The struggle's just started but . . . And there's the

Prime responsible for setting this whole mess in motion," she added as Tobias came out of the Citadel.

"How is Tobias responsible?" Joe asked as the Prime gave them a nod and walked past.

Sid stuck her tongue out at her new boss's back and explained to her bondmate. "It has occurred to me that when he assigned you to find out what I knew about the Tribes, he had more than one motive for sending you."

Joe looked after his leader. "Clever."

Sid knocked her head against his shoulder. "Clever? You ought to be outraged! Somehow he unblocked your shielded memories, so that you and I would interact the way we did, and he stood back to see how far it would go. He could have gotten you killed."

"You're angry at him for my sake? That's so sweet. Tobias *is* a Prime—and if there's one thing I've learned about vampires, it's that you all do what you think is right, even if you don't ask permission."

"He should have let you in on what he intended."

"The Dark Angels work on a need-to-know basis. All I needed to know was what you and I had been to each other."

"I see. It's all right for big, bad Tobias Strahan

to use you, but you get pissed off when I try to protect you," Sid sniffed.

Joe smiled at her. "I don't want you to protect me. I just want you to love me."

"I do. But you're making me angry enough to bite you, and you won't enjoy it."

He pulled her into his arms. "I missed you in every way possible. I love you in every way possible." He kissed her in a way that filled her being with fire. When they were done, Joe added, "And if you ever want to get your memories of Charles unblocked, I know a witch who makes a mean cup of coffee."

Epilogue

December 20
New York, NY

"He will see you." The low-status Prime who spoke didn't try to hide his envy.

Gregor nodded. The idiot had tried to send him away because he had no appointment. Slamming the worm's head onto the top of his desk a few times had convinced the secretary that he should consult his master. He'd just returned with a bloody cut healing on his cheek.

Gregor waited for the cur to open the door to the inner office, then looked around inside while he waited for the door to close. The large room was of the glass-walled-corner-office type that executives were supposed to covet. It was sparsely and expensively furnished. A laptop sat on the glass-topped desk. Only the heavy curtains that covered the windows gave any clue that a vampire occupied the premises.

The Prime studying the computer screen did not look up.

Gregor came forward and placed the small black memory stick on the desk. "The research is complete," he reported. "It's all here. The treatment clinic is set up. You may start the treatments whenever you wish."

The Master Prime finally looked at him. "You perform to expectations."

Gregor nodded in gratitude but waited for the stick after the carrot.

"I hear that you allowed the test animal to escape. I hear that the mortal scientists were captured. I gave no orders for the project to be terminated by you."

"It seemed the right time to dispose of the mortals involved in the drug development," Gregor answered. "We have their data. Our own people are trained. We have a large supply of the Dawn drugs. The Clan morons are easily duped into believing that only the mortal Purists are involved. I made sure that the mortal prisoners they will interrogate also believe that they were the only ones involved. My actions leave the Tribe freedom to maneuver."

"For a while," the Master said after he studied Gregor.

Gregor nodded. "The Clans and the Families still pose a threat to our plans. We will be there to counter whatever they do. I will be there."

"You have done well—even if you do think for yourself too much." The Master gestured toward the door. "You have your life. Get out of my sight."

Discover the darker side of desire.

Pick up a bestselling paranormal romance from Pocket Books!

Kresley Cole
Dark Deeds at Night's Edge
The Immortals After Dark Series

A vampire shunned by his own kind is driven to the edge of madness....where he discovers the ultimate desire.

Jen Holling
My Immortal Protector

Deep in the Scottish Highlands, a reluctant witch is willing to do anything to give up her powers—until she meets the one man who may give her a reason to use them.

Marta Acosta
Happy Hour at Casa Dracula

Come for a drink....Stay for a bite.

Gwyn Cready
Tumbling Through Time

She was a total control freak—until a magical pair of killer heels sends her back in time—and into the arms of the wrong man!

Discover the darker side of passion with these bestselling paranormal romances from Pocket Books!

Kresley Cole
Wicked Deed on a Winter's Night
Immortal enemies…forbidden temptation.

Alexis Morgan
Redeemed in Darkness
She vowed to protect her world from the enemy—
until her enemy turned her world upside down.

Katie MacAlister
Ain't Myth-Behaving
He's a God. A legend. A man of mythic proportions…
And he'll make you long to myth-behave.

Melissa Mayhue
Highland Guardian
For mortals caught in Faeire schemes,
passion can be dangerous…